A GRAND SLAM KIND OF CHRISTMAS

L. B. JOYCE

A Grand Slam Kind of Christmas – 1st edition
Print ISBN: 978-0-9600311-5-3
EBook ISBN: 9781393586494

BY L. B. JOYCE

Holidays in White Oaks Valley - Series
A Grand Slam Kind of Christmas

Twelve Months, Twelve Love Stories - Series
A Million Decembers
For the Love of July
February's Angel
Promise Me November
An Unexpected June
A January to Remember
September's Moonlight Serenade
Goodbye Heartbreak, Hello May

IT'S CHRISTMAS!

When you choose joy,
you feel good.
and when you feel good,
you do good.
This is a reminder to others,
what joy feels like.

May this book give you joy!
Merry Christmas!

CHAPTER 1

Every woman's heart has instructions.
They are written in her eyes,
in her smile,
through her actions, and in her tears.
She only needs to run into someone
who cares enough to read them.
~ Unknown

*J*essie Carter carried the last box to her SUV. She stared down at the packed trunk.

How in the world have you accumulated so much stuff?

When she had made the move to Chicago four years ago, the apartment she and Poppy decided to share was furnished. So, it made little sense her belongings not only filled her trunk, but almost the entire interior space of her SUV as well.

But then again, she had packed up everything she owned, down to the hair ties she found on the bathroom vanity.

Hair ties are a necessity... and look how you're always losing them.

This wasn't a permanent move.

At least this is what she kept telling herself. This was just a temporary reprieve... a break from what she had finally figured out was a no-win situation.

She set the box on the ground and after moving everything around in the trunk; she jammed the box in to fit. Closing her eyes and giving it all she had, she slammed the trunk shut.

Checking her pocket for her keys and breathing a sigh of relief she hadn't locked them in the trunk, she glanced over to where Poppy was standing at the top of the steps. Her hair sticking out all over the place and wearing her ancient and beat up chenille robe, she was a sorry sight on this freezing morning in early December.

Yep, it was what you'd call a cold enough to snow kind of day. In fact, Jessie was pretty sure she had already spotted a few snowflakes drift by while she was loading up her SUV.

Poppy didn't look happy.

No, she looked miserable.

But this was because seven-thirty in the morning wasn't an hour Poppy was familiar with.

Most nights she worked late as a waitress, while during the day she attended Loyola. One year away from graduating with a master's degree in hotel management and hospitality, her dream was to be a cruise ship director.

She was also not a morning person. So, the fact she was now standing out in the freezing cold and half asleep was a huge sacrifice on her part. Especially since she had also made it very clear, more times than Jessie wanted to count, by leaving, Jessie was making the biggest mistake of her life.

As she saw it, Jessie was running away, taking the easy way out. She was a lawyer, for heaven's sake. Shouldn't she be able to come up with a way to prove her innocence? What good was all the experience she had gained over the past five years if she couldn't even use what she'd learned to defend herself?

Her arms wrapped around herself, the frown on Poppy's face grew more pronounced as Jessie came running up the steps to say goodbye.

She pulled back from the hug Jessie tried to give her, giving a frustrated sigh. "Why do I have the feeling, no matter how much you deny it, you won't be coming back? I know your plan is to stay only until your sister has the baby, but clearing all of your belongings from our apartment is sending a whole different message."

Jessie shoved her hands in her pockets, and for a few seconds she was silent.

Then she shook her head. "Okay, I'll admit it... I'm not sure what my plans are, where I'll end up next. But I know one thing... and this is I have no intention of becoming like my sister. Settling down in the small town we grew up in, and opening a cake and coffee shop might be her perfect dream, but it's definitely not the life for me."

Poppy sighed. "I don't know. Right now, it sounds pretty good to me. No stress, a friendly smile everywhere you turn, an old-fashioned kind of Christmas everywhere you look."

Jessie shook her head. "Yeah, maybe this time of year it's not that bad. I know for Crystal it works. But I could never live in a small town again. Not after living in Manhattan and then Chicago. I'd feel like I was wasting my life away."

This small town Jessie was referring to?

This would be Blossom Falls. The town where both she and Crystal were born. It was also where Crystal still lived with her husband, Joe McDonnell, and their ten-year-old son, Jackson.

Jessie didn't agree with Poppy's claim she was running away. She had a perfectly good excuse for returning home. At almost eight and a half months pregnant, Crystal had just been told her blood pressure was much higher than it should be. According to her doctor, to avoid any complications, she needed to take it easy.

For Crystal, this was a big problem. Crystal's Coffee Cakes, a combination coffee shop and specialty coffee cake business, was now up against the busiest time of year.

In the heart of town, it was a favorite of all the local residents.

If you needed a birthday cake or a cake for any other special event, this was your best bet.

Or if you were more interested in only a good cup of coffee and getting the scoop on the town's latest gossip, this was the place to be.

The holiday parties and events popping up around town were bringing in a record amount of business. For Thanksgiving alone, the little shop had turned out more than double the number of their Pumpkin-Praline Coffee Cakes than they had the last year.

Crystal had only one assistant, Marilyn. She was more than willing to take on the extra hours, but one person just wouldn't cut it this time of year.

Last year, Joe had helped whenever he could. But now stationed in Afghanistan, he wasn't expected home until late February.

If all of this wasn't enough, the doctor had also informed Crystal the baby could possibility make an appearance before Christmas.

So, it was understandable she wasn't handling this very well. It also explained the hysterical voice mail she left on Jessie's phone yesterday.

At the time she left her message, Jessie was having problems of her own. Sitting in the office of Joe Dempsey ~ of the Dempsey, Baker and Ross Law Firm ~ she had just been told, because of a conflict of interest between her and the opposing lawyer, she was being removed from her current case. This was a case she had been preparing for over the last six months, twenty-four-seven.

In fact, after a long review of the situation, Joe Dempsey had decided it would be best if she took some time off. A sabbatical of sorts, at least until things blew over. Because, as much as he hated to do this, the firm couldn't afford to lose this case. And if she stayed on, he felt she would only be a reminder of what transpired.

No matter how hard she tried to convince him otherwise, within a half hour, she found herself still in shock and hunched in the corner of the back seat of her taxi. Staring unseeingly out the window, not even the elaborate Christmas decorations on display since Thanksgiving could penetrate the state she was in.

It was when she arrived home and listened to Crystal's message, she decided her plea couldn't have come at a better time.

She was going home…

Fate?

Maybe… maybe, not.

She glanced over at Poppy. "I guess I need time to think about what happened."

She frowned. "I also need to talk to Chad. I'm pretty sure he had a big part in my leaving, since he didn't take our break up very well. He's been nasty ever since."

She sighed, shaking her head. "Unfortunately, since his grandfather was one of the founding partners of the firm, I don't have a chance. It's his word against mine."

Kicking at the pile of dead leaves on the porch, Poppy frowned. "Well, I hope you're not planning to let him get away with this. This is your career he's messing with. Have you called him?"

Jessie shook her head. "I have no intentions of letting him get away with anything. And no, I haven't talked to him. Right now, I'm too afraid of what I might say."

Her mouth twisted in a wry smile. "You know what they say… you have the right to remain silent, anything you say can be used against you in court. The last thing I want is to have him accuse me of threatening him."

She reached over to give Poppy another hug. "Once your exams are over, if you decide not to go home to Michigan, come visit for a few days. I know my sister would welcome you with open arms. She likes nothing better than a full house during the Christmas holidays. The more the merrier is her motto. This could also be your chance to experience what goes on in a small town during the holiday season. I guess everyone should experience this at least once in their life. Both the good and the bad."

She turned and ran down the steps. After she gave Poppy one last wave, she got into her SUV. As she waited for an opening in the traffic, she glanced in her rearview mirror to see Poppy was still on the steps, watching her. Tempted to turn around and go back, she stepped on the gas.

You need to get on the freeway. Out of sight, out of mind, right?

And why this sudden indecision?

She was worried. And why wouldn't she be?

This could be the end of her career. Her intuition was telling her Chad had no plans of letting up on his attacks soon. In fact, she wouldn't put it past him to do whatever he could to ruin her chances of ever practicing law again.

But right now? She needed a break.

She wanted to hide away somewhere. Where she could forget about her career and everything that came along with it.

So, maybe she was the one who needed the small-town Christmas experience, not Poppy.

A wistful smile touched her lips. Her parents had always made Christmas a special holiday for her and Crystal when they were young. And now with both of them gone, Crystal, Joe and Jackson were the only family she had.

What was it they said?

You always need family.

Well, she definitely needed something…

CHAPTER 2

*S*ix hours later, Jessie was driving down Main Street and right into the town of Blossom Falls.

As she took in the festive decorations, she had to hand it to the women's club... when they set out to decorate for the holidays, they did it with a flair.

There was definitely no holding back when it came to Christmas.

Fresh pine trees loaded with lights, were mounted on the street lights, while more lights lined the roof tops and windows of each little shop and store lining the main street.

At one end of the town square, giant candy canes lined both sides of a walkway leading to a huge Christmas tree decorated with giant ornaments and strung with what looked like a million lights. Right next to the tree was a life size gingerbread house, the multi colored candy roof and candy lined windows sparkling with even more lights. The sign on the door listed Santa's schedule. Along with the reminder even though his workload was heavy this time of year he would do his best to listen to everyone's requests.

At the other end of the square, a life size nativity was on display, surrounded by pine trees strung with even more lights.

She could see a booth selling chestnuts was set up in one corner, while another booth nearby was selling hot chocolate and baked goods.

She wondered if any of the bakery being sold was supplied by Crystal's Coffee Cakes. She needed to talk with Crystal about this. Convince her it would be a good advertisement for her business.

She sighed. Unfortunately, this was something she and Crystal argued about all of the time.

In Jessie's mind, she had already envisioned an online site, the business becoming a supplier for grocery stores, maybe even eventually franchising out all across the country. If she invested in a full-scale advertising campaign, the possibilities were endless.

While Crystal claimed she wasn't interested. She didn't have the time nor the funds for something this. She also liked the way things were and was more than happy to keep it the same.

So, this was going to be Jessie's new project. She only needed to persuade Crystal to get on board.

Now driving past Crystal's Coffee Cakes, she glanced over to see business was slow, the shop empty of customers.

It was when her gaze shifted back to the road, she was just in time to see a man had just reached the middle of the cross walk and was now in the path of her moving SUV.

Oh, no, no, no, no...

Sucking in a horrified gasp and gripping the steering wheel as hard as she could, she slammed on the brakes.

CHAPTER 3

May you never be too grown up
to search the skies on Christmas Eve.
~ Anonymous

*M*ax Kirby had arrived in Cleveland only yesterday.

After spending most of the day at the ballpark, meeting what had to be at least a hundred people and knowing for a fact he'd never remember their names, he had crashed, going to bed early last night. To wake up this morning, greeted with blue skies and sunshine.

Well, this is a positive omen. Wasn't Cleveland known for its' lack of sunny days?

Whatever, he'd take it.

After taking advantage of the hotel's complimentary breakfast, thankful no one recognized him, but at the same time disappointed they hadn't, he decided to go for a drive. Maybe this would give him an idea of where he'd like to live.

Yeah, he wanted to see what was available in this town he hoped to call home for the next seven years or more.

As he waited for the heat to come on in his car, he noticed the sun had disappeared. The clouds moving in were definitely hinting at snow.

He sighed. Having grown up in California, before spending the last four years in Minnesota, he had hoped the weather in Cleveland would fall somewhere in between.

Not happening, is it? The below freezing temperatures and snow are leaning more towards what you'd expect of Minnesota.

Proof of this was the snowflake drifting down onto the windshield. When this was followed by another and then yet another, he shook his head.

He had mixed feelings about this move to Cleveland.

Yeah, his signed contract, with the promise of more money than he could possibly spend, had him feeling more than grateful. But that he was now considered one of most sought out professional baseball players, something he'd worked so hard at ever since he was just a kid, still felt more like a dream than reality.

And though he had never regretted the hard work involved, he hadn't prepared himself for everything else that came with the job. Like the constant traveling, the trade rumors always swirling in the background. And most importantly, trusting his decisions regarding the future. His future.

Like his dad had so eloquently phrased it, he had to grow up pretty fast.

Never had he imagined, in less than twenty-four hours after he became a free agent, Cleveland would give him an offer he would've been crazy to refuse. And now, for the first time since he embarked on this whirlwind climb, he felt like he'd finally landed where he was meant to be.

But this brought on big changes in his life. Having grown comfortable with his life in Minnesota, it had been hard to leave behind the many friends he'd made. Along with his girlfriend, Mandy.

At least you thought she was your girlfriend…maybe even more. You had even gone as far as thinking about sharing a future together.

Yeah, he had come so close to dropping the big one. You know... the will you marry me bombshell. But this all flew out the window when she broke up with him less than a month before he signed with Cleveland. Then, wasting no time, she got engaged to one of the other guys on the Minnesota team, leaving him more bewildered than angry.

He told himself this was for the best. Marriage was a commitment he took seriously, a vow he wanted to honor. When he finally took that big step, he wanted it to last. He had his parents to thank for this. He wanted what they had. Married for over thirty years, they were still very much in love.

This reminded him he needed to return his mother's call about Christmas. Even after the craziness that comes from raising five children, she was never happier than when they all came together for the holidays.

She'd made it perfectly clear his move to Cleveland wasn't an excuse not to come home for Christmas. And since his schedule was pretty open until he reported for spring training in February, this would be the perfect time to reconnect with family.

He smiled, shaking his head. A wild group, his brothers and sisters. They were all so different, in so many ways.

Two years younger, his twin brothers, Richard and David, co-owned an advertising business in the same town the family had lived since his parents met in high school. David was the creative genius of the company, while Richard handled the finance and marketing end. They both claimed they were too busy building up the business to even think of getting involved in a relationship.

His youngest sister, Christy, was a personal trainer. He could vouch for how good she was. She was dating a friend of his from high school, Sam Bowers. He also played professional ball, but in California.

His older sister Susie was a pediatrician. She lived in Boston with her husband Ben, who was an orthopedic surgeon. They had three girls, Kellie, Mandi and Rachel. Every time he saw her,

Susie claimed she and Ben were going to slow down, spend more time with the girls, take more time off. But their dedication to their work told Max this probably wouldn't be happening soon.

The snow was now coming down more steadily, giving him that snow globe feeling. Following the winding road he was on, not a clue where he was, he slowed down to read the sign posted on the side of the road.

Welcome to Blossom Falls
A Small Town with a Big Heart.
Pop. 4003
Est. 1837

He drove on until he came to a stop sign. His right turn put him on Main Street, where another sign indicated the center of town was less than a mile down the road.

Admiring the impressive assortment of well-kept Victorian-style homes he passed, he found himself at the top of a steep hill. For a long moment, he gazed down at the bustling, almost idyllic scene on display in front of him.

Holy smokes, where the heck are you?

Had he somehow entered another place and time?

He was seriously beginning to think this was what happened. Given that the scene now in front of him wasn't like anything he'd ever seen before.

He drove down to the bottom of the hill, stopping at the intersection to let a horse pulled carriage pass by in front of him. It was only after the car behind him gave a short beep, he continued down Main Street and into town.

Driving slowly, he took it all in. From what he could see, there was every kind of shop imaginable... gifts for the home, women's apparel, stationary, men's clothing, shoes, boots, beauty products, perfumes and more. There was also a great variety of places to eat and drink. Whether it be coffee, wine, fine dining or the comfort of a home cooked meal, there was a place to appease your palette.

Deciding it might be fun to do a little exploring, he pulled into the first available parking space he saw and shut off the ignition. After yanking on his knit hat and grabbing his gloves, a small café right across the street caught his eye. This bringing on a sudden need for a cup of hot coffee, he headed in that direction.

He was halfway through the cross walk when he heard the loud screech of brakes.

A way too close for comfort kind of screech.

He froze.

After a few seconds had passed, and he realized he was still alive and miraculously all in one piece, he let out the breath he'd been holding.

He glanced over at the SUV, and right into the eyes of the driver that had come within inches of hitting him. A woman, she was glaring at him over the steering wheel she was clutching in her hands. From what he could see, she was furious. So much more than she should be under the circumstances.

Rooted to the spot, he stared back at her. He was confused. Was she angry at him? If so, why?

If anyone had the right to be mad, shouldn't it be you?

Considering the loud screech from her sudden stop, one would think Jessie had been traveling a hundred miles an hour, if not more. The jarring sound was loud enough to have everyone stop what they were doing to see what was going on.

Great, just great… you know how the people in Blossom Falls feel about speeding in town. They pride themselves on ticketing jay-walkers, if only to teach a lesson.

Her heart thundering in her chest, she rested her forehead on the steering wheel. After she took a moment to get herself together, she lifted her head.

Her eyes met those of the man she'd almost run over. And for some insane reason, the inquiring look he sent her, no doubt expecting an apology of some kind, made her furious.

She sent him her most threatening look. The look she used in the courtroom when the witness wasn't cooperating. When this didn't seem to phase him, this irked her even more.

Now Jessie knew she had no reason to be angry. If anything, she should thank her lucky stars she hadn't hit him. She was the one at fault, not him. He wasn't jay-walking. And even if he was, as a pedestrian, he had the right of way.

If anyone should know this, it would be you. And if anyone were to be angry, it should be him.

This meant she needed to send him a wave or smile... or something. But for some odd reason, she couldn't.

What's your problem?

She didn't know why she felt like this, but there was something about this man that irritated her. Maybe it was the way he carried himself. Confident, his shoulders thrown back, his stride so sure and purposeful.

She saw this as arrogant, controlling.

It didn't help he was also extremely attractive. His dark, slightly windblown hair, designer ski jacket and hiking boots sent out the vibes he was a man of the world. Whether it was off to the ski slopes in the winter or wine country in the summer, he would always be ready for the next new adventure.

She frowned. She'd be willing to bet he was here to meet up with his picture-perfect girlfriend for dinner. He definitely wasn't married.

Nope, he wasn't ready yet to settle down.

Yes, there was no doubt about it, he was the type of man who was out of bounds, best left alone.

A confused shake of his head, Max turned and continued across the street. He couldn't remember the last time a woman had given him such a look. Whatever had made her so angry, and he'd be willing to bet it had nothing to do with him, it would be in his best interest to ignore her and move on.

An angry woman was the one thing that scared him. Fortunately, he had come up against one only two or three times in his life, but this was more than enough.

It was while he was waiting for a crying toddler to be picked up from the path in front of him, for some insane reason, he turned around to see if the woman was still there.

She was.

And she was watching him.

Once again, their eyes met, and after what he'd describe as a half frown, half smile flashing across her face, she sent him a wave and drove off.

Now he was more bewildered than ever.

Do you think she lives here?

He shook his head. Nah, he doubted this.

But say she did... what if the two of you were to meet again?

But this is crazy... why would he want to see her again?

Feeling unsettled, blaming this on his near brush with death, he walked even faster, the need for that cup of coffee now even more urgent.

Crystal's Coffee Cakes.

He gazed up at the sign hanging above the door. It was a name that fit right in with everything else he'd seen so far in this picture perfect little town.

Well... everything except the woman who tried to kill you.

His hand on the door handle, he paused. Call him crazy, but there was also one more thing he couldn't stop thinking about. And that he was even thinking this, made little sense.

He wondered... was it possible to have eyes that blue?

Again, why are you even still thinking about her?

He pushed open the door.

It was time to move on.

As Jessie drove away, it was a struggle not to look back, maybe catch another glimpse of Mr. Perfect, this the nickname she gave him.

Not perfect for her, of course. Oh, no... if you remember, she'd already decided she didn't like him. But if she were to run into him again—and yes, she realized this was a terrible choice of words since this is what she already almost did—she still wouldn't like him.

Right?

She groaned, dragging her hand through her hair. She was going to blame her befuddled state on the long day she'd had. On the road now for almost seven hours, her only stops for gas and coffee, she was not only tired, but hungry, too.

Yeah... this was her excuse. Once she got to Crystal's, took a shower, and had something to eat, she'd feel more like herself.

She just needed to slow down a little, stop thinking so much.

Then everything would be all right.

CHAPTER 4

*a*s soon as Max walked into Crystal's Coffee Cakes, he was transported right back to his childhood and the times he'd spent with his grandparents.

As you can imagine, with five kids in the family, a weekend spent alone with them had been a special treat.

The kitchen had been his grandmother's favorite room in the house, where it always smelled like a bakery because of the huge jar of cinnamon she kept on the stove. Adding it to almost everything she made, she claimed even a pinch or two made a recipe come to life.

He'd spent hours with her in that kitchen, the time they shared, leaving him with some of the best memories of his childhood.

He smiled as he gazed around at the small space. The décor was like something out of a movie. The walls were wallpapered in a red and white checkered pattern and red tablecloths covered the three small tables lined up next to the windows.

At first glance, it appeared as though he was the only one in the shop. Thinking everyone must be in the back, he pulled off his hat and stuffed it in his pocket. Then he meandered over to the counter to look at the bakery in the display case.

According to what *was* printed out on the blackboard behind the counter, these were the flavors of the day.

Cinnamon Raisin Coffee Cake
Cinnamon Apple Coffee Cake
Cinnamon Cheesecake Coffee Cake
Cinnamon S'More Coffee Cake

This assortment of cakes was available in three sizes — the bundt coffee cake, a standard loaf and the ever so popular mini coffee cakes.

At least this was what was written on the blackboard.

Still in no hurry, Max studied the drink menu posted on the wall behind the counter. There seemed to be as many choices of coffee flavors as there were cakes.

This now had him both hungry and thirsty, his stomach giving a growl in anticipation.

He cleared his throat. "Hello? Is anyone here?"

At first this was met with silence. Then he heard what sounded like someone mumbling in the back room.

If he wasn't mistaken, it was a woman.

Suddenly on alert, he dragged his hand through his hair.

Geeez… why do you have a bad feeling about this?

He didn't know if he was up to meeting any of the other women in this town. Not after his encounter with the woman who almost mowed him down in broad daylight .

But again, he was hungry… and coffee would really hit the spot right now.

After clearing his throat, he called out again. "Hey, hello… are you open for business?"

He finally received a response. A very faint one.

"I think I could use some help?"

Well, who was he to turn down a damsel in distress?

Slowly skirting around the counter, he cautiously made his way into the back room.

A woman, obviously very pregnant was sitting on the floor. Leaning against the refrigerator with her eyes closed, she looked completely done in.

He was next to her in a flash. "Are you okay? What happened? Should I call the EMS?"

Granted, he may have over-reacted, but the woman looked like she was about to go into labor any minute.

And he knew nothing... *absolutely nothing* about what procedure to follow when a woman was about to give birth.

He vaguely remembered watching a movie where this was about to happen. But the only thing that stuck with him was the request for hot water and towels. What these were for, he couldn't tell you. And he wasn't too sure if he really wanted to know.

At least not now, you don't.

This was when he saw her name embroidered on her shirt... Crystal.

Ah... she must be the owner.

He took a deep breath.

"Crystal, whatever you want me to do, just tell me. But, no matter what, I won't leave you."

She opened her eyes only a crack and for what felt like forever, she studied him. Then she sighed. "Isn't this typical of my kind of luck? Every woman dreams about how once in her life, a handsome and sexy man comes to her rescue, sweeping her up off her feet and whisking her away from danger."

Her smile was wistful. "And of course, when this happens to me?"

She began counting off on her fingers. "One, I'm already married. Two, I'm pregnant and weigh a ton. And three? I'm certainly not looking my best."

At first, he said nothing. He was still having a little bit of a hard time getting over the one word she used to describe him.

Sexy? She thinks you're sexy? Hmm...

A smile tweaked the corner of his mouth. This was a new one

for him. He'd been referred to as athletic, rugged, or maybe even going as far as handsome, but never... *no, never...* had a woman told him she thought he was sexy.

And he liked it.

He felt confident, yet at the same time, sort of reckless. Wild and dangerous, even...

He gave her one of his best grins. "Out of all the pregnant women I've run into lately, you are by far the most beautiful of all. Now please, tell me... are you okay? Do I need to call for help?"

She patted the floor next to her. "Here, sit down next to me. I'm fine. Believe it or not, it was a pretty graceful fall. And now, I only need a few minutes to recoup. Then you should be able to help me up. You appear to be more than strong enough."

Deciding it was probably best not to argue with a woman in her condition, he did as she asked.

She smiled over at him. "So, tell me... what's your name? Are you just visiting? Because I have a feeling you aren't from around here. I would've recognized you if you were."

She peered more closely at him. "Though you do look sort of familiar." Her eyes lit up. "Are you a doctor of some kind? Maybe I saw you advertised in one of these coupon circulars we get in the mail?"

He chuckled, shaking his head. "In answer to all of your questions, my name is Max, short for Maxwell and named after my grandfather. I'm not from around here, but in the process of moving because my career brought me here. And, I'm definitely not a doctor."

He shook his head. "I get kind of queasy when it comes to that kind of thing. I couldn't even dissect a frog in my high school biology class. I had to leave the room."

He shook his head just thinking about this. His friends still took every chance they could to razz him about this.

She gave a slow nod. "So, you're planning to move here... somewhere around Cleveland. Is your job in the city?"

He nodded. "Yes, but I'm ready to give up city living. I'd like some grass, trees, a space-between-neighbors-kind-of-place. I grew up in the Napa Valley area of California and I miss that kind of life."

She was shaking her head. "Oh dear, you do realize you're in Ohio, don't you? You might want to think of changing your requirements to apple orchards and lake-side living. Not that we don't have a lot of great places to live outside of the city. So, you should be able to find something."

She frowned. "My sister Jessie lives in Chicago. I wish she'd get tired of city life. She's coming for Christmas to help out since my husband won't be home until January."

At his raised eyebrow, she sighed. "He's in Afghanistan, won't be home until February."

He nodded. "Wow... must be hard. But you must also be so proud."

She shrugged. "It's been hard, being pregnant and all. But this doesn't mean I don't support him. Because I do... totally." She grinned. "And, this time, our ten-year-old son Jackson took his father very seriously when he told him he had to be the man of the house."

After a short silence, she looked over at him. "I know we don't have the ocean, but we do have Lake Erie, along with our share of beautiful sunsets. And as far as wineries go, we're still new to this growing-grapes-for-wine thing. But we do like to drink it now and then."

Her eyes lit up again. "And don't forget the change of the seasons."

"Woooooo Hoooooo... Crystal, where are you? I need a cake."

A look of panic on her face, Crystal began struggling to get off the floor. "Oh, no... it's Robin Miller. I forgot... she sent a text she'd be stopping by to pick up a cake. She's the town gossip. She graduated with Jessie and I swear, even though she's over thirty years younger, she's a double for Mrs. Kravitz on Bewitched."

At his blank look, she laughed. "Not familiar with the show, are you? Let's just say she takes gossip to a whole new level."

Max had quickly jumped up from the floor and holding out his hands to her, between the two of them, she was finally standing.

She sent him a wry smile. "Thanks. I'm sure humoring a woman in her last stages of pregnancy wasn't at the top of your list of things to do today, so I really appreciate your help. Come on, I want you to pick out a mini cake. And a coffee, too. It's on me. It's the least I can do to repay you."

Before he could answer she had already hurried into the shop.

Max sauntered in after her, heading right over to the display case. He was going to make his choice and leave. After what Crystal told him about this Robin Miller, he wanted nothing to do with her. He certainly didn't want to wind up as the subject of her latest gossip.

But it immediately became clear Robin wasn't going to let him get off this easily. She came over to him, holding out her hand. "Well, hello there… I'm Robin Miller. Are you new in town? Because I'm darn sure if we'd crossed paths before, I'd remember you."

She leaned in even closer, the scent of her perfume so over-powering, he stepped back to catch his breath.

She spoke in an exaggerated whisper. "Whatever Crystal told you about me, I assure you, none of it's true. The Carter girls have always been jealous of us Miller girls." She gave an empathetic nod. "Yes, believe it or not, there are two of us."

She held her arms out. "Can you imagine? All this, times two. I have a twin sister who now lives in Phoenix. Her name is Starling."

He raised an eyebrow. "Starling?"

She nodded. "Yes, you heard right. My mother was, and still is, a fan of all feathered creatures, big and small."

Rolling her eyes, Crystal came to his rescue. "For heaven's

sake, Robin... leave the poor guy alone. He was nice enough to help me out a moment ago, and I'm pretty sure he wants his cake and coffee so he can beat it out of here and get on with his life."

Her hands on her hips, she shook her head. "And for the hundredth time, Jessie and I aren't jealous of you and Starling... never was, not now, and never will be."

She turned to Max. "Now, what have you decided on?"

He smiled at her. "The Cinnamon Apple and a regular black coffee. I like my coffee straight up."

Robin winked at him. "I'm not surprised. You come across as a man who likes everything no frills. If you know what I mean."

This had Max almost grabbing the coffee and bag with the mini coffee cake right out of Crystal's hands.

You've gotta get out of here, because who knows what she'll come up with next?

Throwing a twenty-dollar bill on the counter he turned and headed for the door.

"Hey, wait... remember, it's my treat."

He turned to see Crystal waving the bill at him. He shook his head. "Nope, I insist on paying. I've got a lot to be thankful for, a lot to celebrate. So, I want to share." He waved. "Take it easy, okay?"

He hadn't even reached the door before Robin began firing all of these questions at Crystal. "Celebrate? I wonder what he's celebrating? Maybe he's getting married? I noticed he wasn't wearing a ring, so he must be single. I must say, there's something intriguing about him. He's hot, that's for sure. And sexy as all get out."

Replenishing the cakes in the display case, Crystal wasn't even listening to her. But this didn't bother Robin. Everyone always ignored her. So, if she had something to say, she kept right on talking. "He looks so darn familiar. Maybe he's an actor or celebrity of some kind? I don't see him as the football player type. Did he tell you where he was from? Or why he's even here?"

She sent Crystal a curious look. "What did you mean when you said he helped you out? Helped you out with what?"

Closing the door to the display case, Crystal massaged her aching back. She wasn't in the mood to listen to any of Robin's theories right now. She wanted to go home. Where she could sit down and put her feet up.

She began wiping the counter. "He offered to pick up something for me in the back room." She gave a huge sigh. "I can't wait until Joe finally comes home. There's something about having a man around. Someone you can count on to make everything a little easier."

She smiled. "But this guy? Who knows if we'll ever see him again? He did seem nice, though, didn't he?"

Before Robin could even open her mouth to answer, she cut her off. "So, you came in for a cake? What kind? You'll have to tell me again, because I'm afraid I forgot. Blame it on being pregnant. At this point I'm lucky if I remember my name."

She pulled out a cake box and began putting it together. "Let's get you taken care of so I can close up. I'm sure you have a lot going on and want to get home, too. Right?"

This always worked at getting Robin out of the shop. She prided herself on her busy schedule, something she was always quick to remind everyone about.

Sure enough, she began checking out the cakes, the mysterious man forgotten.

This didn't mean she wasn't going to look into this later.

She'd swear she knew him from somewhere.

Max found a bench in a less crowded part of the square, where he finished off the mini coffee cake and his coffee in record time. He wished he had bought more than one, the cake was that good.

He checked his phone. Confronted with a long line of texts, he shut it off and stuffed it back in his pocket. Fueled by the cake and coffee, he decided he was going to check out more of the town before he left.

He hauled himself off the bench. The texts could wait.

CHAPTER 5

Keep calm. Keep jingling on.
~ Anonymous

*J*essie grabbed her suitcase and garment bag out of the backseat of her SUV and made her way over to the side door of the small bungalow that was Crystal and Joe's home. This took her right into the kitchen.

Jumping up from his place at the kitchen table, where he was doing his homework, Jackson came running over to hug her, bags and all. "Aunt Jessie, you made it."

She grinned and dropping everything to the floor, she gave him a big hug. "Yes, I finally made it. And how is my favorite nephew?"

"Aunt Jessie... you always say that. I'm your only nephew, remember?"

She laughed, giving him another hug. "Yes, so this still means you're my favorite, right?"

She watched as he began dragging her suitcase and garment bag down the hall to take them up to the guest room.

Nora, the babysitter Crystal had hired to take care of Jackson after school, began gathering up her notebooks. A senior in high school, Crystal swore she didn't know what she'd do without her.

Jessie shook her head. "Don't tell me Crystal is at the shop. I almost stopped there, but thought she'd be home. Isn't she supposed to be taking it easy?"

Nora shrugged "You know how she is... she listens to no one. I'm glad you came to help out. I swear, if she doesn't slow down, she's going to have the baby any day now." She grinned. "My mom's opinion, not mine."

She grabbed her phone off the table. "This is her now." After she read the text, she smiled over at Jessie. "She's closing up right now. So, since you're here, I'm going to take off. I need to run a few errands. See ya." She was gone before Jessie even had a chance to say goodbye.

Jackson came back into the kitchen. "Do you have any more stuff to bring in? If you do, I'm your man. Dad told me he's counting on me to I help with all of the heavy lifting and stuff." He sent her a critical glance. "Even though you're not having a baby, I guess I should help you, too."

Reaching over to ruffle his hair, she smiled. "I can definitely use your help. Get your coat and boots on, because it's snowing again." She glanced around the kitchen. "Then we'll try to figure out what's for dinner before your mom gets here."

"Uh, oh... the lasagna." He sent her a worried look. "I forgot. It needs to be heated up and it's still in the refrigerator."

Jessie took the lasagna out of the refrigerator, popped it in the oven and set the temperature.

She smiled at him. "There ya go. We're all set. Now let's get the rest of my stuff."

Jessie put what remained of the lasagna in the refrigerator. In the kitchen and cleaning up, she could hear Crystal laughing at something Jackson said. They were in the living room, watching TV.

She was proud of how she had managed to evade Crystal's numerous questions during dinner. The details about her break up with Chad were first and foremost on Crystal's list, followed by her concern over what happened at the firm to have Jessie leave so abruptly.

But Jessie didn't want to talk about any of this... not yet.

With Chad, it didn't matter. Because as far as she was concerned, they were done. For good. In fact, she had now accepted there hadn't really been anything between them in the first place.

He had used her, plain and simple. His only interest in her had been what she could do to make him look good.

Yeah, with you doing all the work. To have him show up, ready to go and wearing another one of his expensive and hand tailored suits he's so proud of.

Yep, he was history. Done. Finished. Forever.

But her job? This was a whole different situation. It bothered her that she hadn't been able to get an explanation of what really happened. It had to be pretty serious for the firm to want her out of the picture. It just didn't made sense.

Somehow, she was going to get to the bottom of this, one way or the other.

After staring down at the pattern of frolicking puppies and kittens on the dish towel, she finally folded it and draped it over the sink. Topping off the wine in her glass, the wine Crystal insisted she'd bought just for her, she went to join her and Jackson in the living room.

They were both on the sofa, Crystal's feet propped up on extra pillows she had piled on the ottoman.

She smiled at Jessie. "Thanks for cleaning up."

Curling up in the chair by fireplace, Jessie rested her head against the back. "You're welcome. There really wasn't a lot of dishes and you did feed me. So, it's the least I could do."

She reached into her pocket and pulling out a phone, she tossed it to Crystal. "Before I forget, here's your phone. You left it on the table. I think someone might have left a message... a Susan Hillard, or something like that."

For a few seconds, Crystal stared at her.

Then, a horrified expression coming over her face, she began struggling to get off the sofa. "*Oh, my God...* the Women's Club luncheon cakes. I forgot all about them. I was going to get them ready to go when I tripped and fell on the floor—"

Jessie dove out of her chair to grab onto her, gently pushing her back on the sofa. "Whoa... take it easy. And what's this, you fell?"

Crystal groaned, waving her away. "Don't worry, I'm fine. But I can't believe I forgot. Susan—she's the president of the women's club—she asked me to deliver the cakes tonight because they want to gift wrap the boxes. They didn't think they'd have time tomorrow morning before the luncheon."

She attempted to get off the sofa again. "I need to deliver the cakes right now."

Jessie put her hands on her shoulders and looked directly into her face. "You're not going anywhere. You are going to sit right here and be good. I will take care of the cakes. But, Crissy... seriously? What were you thinking? Why did you take on such a big order?"

Crystal frowned. "Give me a little credit here, the order was placed before I even knew I was pregnant. But, are you sure you don't mind doing this? It's such a big order...thirty cakes."

Incredulous, Jessie stared at her. "Thirty? Why so many? This is a women's luncheon, right? Not a full-blown banquet."

Crystal nodded. "Yeah, I know. It's a lot of cakes. I guess they're giving most of them away. I should have asked Max to help me."

Jessie peered at her, wondering if this fall she'd mentioned may have addled her brain. "Max? Who is Max?"

Leaning back in the cushions, Crystal closed her eyes. "Oh, he was this really nice guy who came in the shop right after I slipped and fell."

At Jessie's murderous look, she shook her head. "It was no big deal. Not even what you'd call a fall. I slid right down against the refrigerator. But I couldn't get up. So, when I heard someone calling out from the shop, I asked him to come into the back room."

She started to giggle. "The poor guy. I made him sit on the floor with me and we had such a nice chat." She frowned. "But then Robin came into the shop for an order."

Jessie shook her head. "Definitely a good way to ruin your day. So, what happened with this Max?"

"He left. But only after I treated him to his choice of mini cake and a coffee. He really was such a nice guy. Though he seemed sort of lonely. I never found out what he does for a living, only that he was transferred here and was looking for a place to live."

She sighed. "I think Robin scared him half to death. He grabbed the cake and coffee right out of my hand before he practically sprinted out the door. We both thought he looked familiar. Robin thought he was a celebrity. She also thought he was hot. Or sexy was the word she used..."

She smiled. "He had nice eyes. And such a gentleman. He left a twenty for the coffee and cake. When I tried to give it back, he made the comment he had a lot to celebrate, a lot to be thankful for. I wonder what this was?"

She shrugged. "Oh well, he's probably far gone by now." She shot Jessie a worried look. "But the cakes... they need to be delivered. The boxes are in the freezer, all marked with a W. I know the women's club meeting starts at eight and it is almost seven now. Are you sure you don't want me to—"

Already putting on her coat, Jessie shook her head. "No, what I want, is for you to stop worrying and relax. I am perfectly capable of handling this."

She nodded over towards the other end of the sofa where Jackson was all curled up and fast asleep. "It looks like Jackson is out. Just leave him there and I'll get him to bed when I get back."

The worried look still on her face, Crystal nodded. "Okay, but please be careful. And be safe."

Jessie grinned back at her as she left the room.

"Come on, Crystal, this is Blossom Falls... what could possibly happen?"

CHAPTER 6

*T*he town square was almost empty of visitors when Jessie pulled her SUV in front of Crystal's Coffee Cakes. After she unlocked the door, she slipped inside the dark shop and headed straight to the back room without turning on the light. She didn't want anyone to think they were open.

She opened the freezer door, and after giving a big groan at the sight of all the cake boxes marked with a W, she began loading them on a cart.

After she wheeled the cart outside, she began searching her pockets for her keys.

They were nowhere to be found. Thinking she must have left them inside, she went back in to look.

Five minutes later, still searching, she was trying not to panic.

After Max had checked out the whole town, even going as far to study all of the home for sale listings posted in the window of the local real estate office, he was not only freezing, he was also hungry again.

It felt like the temperature had dipped ten degrees or more. It had also started to snow… a fine, stinging snow. A burger and a beer sounding like a good idea, he had decided to stop into a little sports bar he'd passed earlier.

Now, leaving the bar, he was greeted by darkness. It was also a lot colder. This explained why the square was so empty.

Putting his hat on, his collar up and pulling on his gloves, he headed for his car. He was eager to get back to his hotel. He had spent more time hanging around this little town than he'd planned. Locked into his contract for the next seven years, he needed to quit fooling around and get serious about finding a place to live. Put down some roots, find a place to call his own.

Yeah, you're ready to settle down. Never thought you'd be saying this, but you are.

This was what was on his mind as he began walking towards the infamous crosswalk. Shaking his head, thinking about his encounter earlier with, what he now thought of her as the crazy woman, he glanced over at Crystal's Coffee Cakes.

He slowed his pace.

Hmm… what's this?

The door to the little shop was partially open, a pile of boxes stacked right outside. Since the interior of the shop was dark, an indication it was closed for the day, this had him wondering if something was wrong.

Striding over to the shop, he peered into the dark interior. He could see there was a light on in the back room.

Was Crystal working late? Maybe she fell again?

Silently entering the shop, he slowly made his way towards the back room.

Later, when he thought about what happened next, he wondered why he hadn't even thought about calling out to announce his presence.

He decided the cold had obviously frozen his brain.

This could be the only reason for why he did what he did.

Because why else would he have gone into high gear, sprinting over to throw open the door? To then charge into the back room like an out-of-control and complete idiot?

So, he really only had himself to blame for what happened next.

Jessie had finally found her keys, on the floor and under the counter, when she heard a sound behind her.

She whirled around to immediately freeze in place.

A man came to an abrupt halt in front of her. With his hat pulled down and his collar up, she could only see his eyes.

Oh, my God… oh, my God… oh, my God…

This was the only thing that came out of her mouth and unfortunately, only in a whisper.

For one very long moment, they both didn't move.

Then her adrenaline finally jumping into gear, she grabbed a potholder from the counter. Letting out a loud shriek, she began swinging the potholder at his head. This pushed his hat down even further, completely covering his eyes.

She began yelling like a madwoman. *"Go away… get out of here… now."*

Max was completely unprepared for this. He honestly had no idea he looked like an extremely dangerous intruder who was up to no good.

It also didn't help he was in shock. This was because when she had turned to face him, he immediately recognized her.

Yes, she was none other than, the crazy woman who had almost run him over in the crosswalk.

You've gotta be kidding… she is the absolute last person you want to see.

He couldn't see a darn thing. Shielding his face with his arms, while trying to pull his hat off at the same time, he kept backing up in an attempt to avoid her swings with the potholder. His voice came out in a muffled roar. "Stop it! I am not going to hurt you. I'm only here to make sure everything is all right. I thought you were Crystal."

It was Crystal's name that finally had Jessie ending her

attack. Even though she still held on to the potholder, clutching it to her chest.

He could see she was shaking. He groaned.

Oh no... now look what you've done.

Breathing hard and staring at each other, for a few long moments, they didn't move.

Then she suddenly dropped her arms to her sides, a look of complete disbelief on her face.

Now that she could see his face?

Please, no... The man in the crosswalk? How did he know you were here?

Her heart pounding in her chest and one eye on the door, gaging a possible escape, she began to back away from him. Very slowly she did this, her whisper coming out loud in the tense silence between them. "Why are you here? If it's because of what happened... you know, the minor little incident at the cross-walk... I apologize."

Then, she just couldn't help it... she gave a huffy sigh. "Even though that was almost as much your fault as it was mine. Did you even bother to look both ways before you went strutting across the street? As if you had no care in the world? Or, did you think, because of your expensive clothing and good looks, you're entitled to preferential treatment?"

Incredulous, he stared at her.

Strutting? You don't strut. Isn't that what peacocks do? To show off their feathers?

Nope...

You. Do. Not. Strut.

Now a little angry, he moved closer. "Now wait a minute. First of all, I don't strut. I never have and never will. Secondly, what I wear and my looks are none of your concern."

Even though he was a little flattered she thought he looked good.

Yeah, this town is really starting to grow on you with all these compliments you've been getting.

He crossed his arms over his chest. *"Hmm...* maybe instead of taking the time to check me out, you should've been paying more attention to your driving?"

He narrowed his eyes. "You do know pedestrians have the right of way, don't you? In fact, it's a law."

"Of course, I know that. I'm a—" She clamped her mouth shut. She saw no reason to tell him anything. Least of all, that she was a lawyer. This would probably only bring on a lecture about her and lawyers in general. And she wasn't in the mood.

Leaning back against the counter, she waved her hand in dismissal. "Yeah, again, I'm sorry about that. But it's not like I would've hit you. I stopped in time, didn't I? And you were able to go on your merry way, no worse for the wear."

She kept an eye on him the entire time she was talking. At the same time, she began patting the counter behind her, searching for a better weapon.

You know, just in case.

But the only thing her fingers came in contact with was another potholder.

She groaned.

Well, this certainly isn't going to be of any help, is it?

But she could see he seemed to be totally frustrated by what she said. And, this immediately had a calming effect on her. Now she would be able to jump right in with her let's-be-friends-mode of attack, a move she'd perfected and one she was quite proud of.

Proven to be a valuable tool in the courtroom, it should certainly work for you now.

Her confidence restored, but still not ready to let go of the potholder, she looked him right in the eye. "So, tell me... how do you know Crystal?"

But before he could even respond, recognition dawned on her face. *"Oh my God...* you're the guy who came to her rescue when she fell today. Your name is Mark... or something like that. And this must have happened right after I almost..."

Her voice trailed off. There was no need to bring that up again. She had already apologized. Why give him the chance to pile on the guilt?

He gave her a wry smile. "Max… not Mark. My name is Max. And yes, it was right after our little run in that I met your sister. This is the reason I'm now here. I was walking to my car and I saw the door to the shop was open. Along with quite a few boxes stacked up outside. Since the shop was all dark, I thought this looked suspicious and decided to check it out."

He shrugged. "I wanted to make sure, if it was Crystal here in the shop, she hadn't fallen again. Or, if she was working late, I could help her out. It must be hard, being so pregnant while her husband is away on duty."

A grin suddenly twitching the corner of his mouth, he nodded towards the potholder in her hand. "So, you can put away your weapon. And you won't need the other one I see you've found on the counter. Trust me, I'm one of the good guys."

He shook his head, still grinning. "And after what conspired earlier? Why would I even think of trying to get close to you? I still have a lot of living to do, and have no plan of jeopardizing this by falling under your attack."

She stilled, her whole body shifting into an attack mode. Then, after glancing down at the potholder, she casually tossed it back on the counter. She shrugged. "There… are you happy? I've laid down my weapon and have no plans of coming at you again, either by driving or wielding a potholder."

She grew silent, staring down at her hands. His reason for coming into the shop had her feeling guilty.

Intrigued, he waited. He had the feeling she had more to say.

Sure enough, she gave a long dramatic sigh. "All right, so maybe I may have over re-acted. But do you blame me? You came charging in here, your face all hidden and acting like some kind of demented fugitive, ready to attack. So why wouldn't I think the worst?"

Then she proceeded to turn everything around, putting all of the blame on him. "What were you thinking? I'm surprised you didn't tackle me and throw me to the ground—" She pressed her lips together, suddenly afraid of what might come out of her mouth next. No doubt it wouldn't be good.

Trying to hide his smile, Max had moved a little closer. "*Ah... so this is what you actually think, huh? And after pinning you to the floor? The crazy fugitive that I am, what would my next move be? Tie you up so I could make off with all of Crystal's coffee cakes?*"

He slapped his hand to his forehead. "*Ah... but I guess I wouldn't know, would I? Since I'm not a fugitive.*"

Now he was making fun of her? She tossed her head, her eyes flashing with anger. "Sure, go ahead... make a joke about it."

Fascinated, he watched a change come over her. No longer angry, she was pouting. "It really wasn't funny. You scared me."

He studied her, shaking his head. Honestly, this woman could flip from one emotion to the other faster than anyone he knew. And even more so in her eyes.

Especially in her eyes. She couldn't hide her feelings even if she tried. At least not with you.

He sighed. Again, he had the distinct feeling this anger inside of her wasn't all because of him. Something, or maybe someone, had messed up her life pretty good, driving her to this state.

And truth be told? He'd had enough.

He wasn't a confrontational kind of guy. So, all these accusations flying back and forth between them made him uncomfortable. That the majority of this anger was directed at him, made it even worse.

So, what do you want to do about it?

He couldn't believe he was even thinking this, but he wanted to erase the slate and start over. He wanted to sit down with her, maybe even share a glass of wine together. They would talk of ordinary things, find out more about each other. Then maybe he'd get a smile out of her, maybe even go as far as to make her laugh.

But most of all, he wanted a chance to spend more time with her. If only so he could gaze into her eyes. Eyes by far the most beautiful he had ever seen. They were like a magnet, drawing him in. And somewhere, deep in the amazing blue that they were, he had a feeling they held the promise of what he had been looking for in his life.

And now you think the answer to what you want is in her eyes? Wait a minute... how did you come up with this?

During these last few minutes they'd spent together, he'd noticed her eyes weren't only blue, they were a combination of so many different shades of blue depending on her mood. He'd witnessed the flash of deep sapphire brought on because of anger. Or how they would turn into deep pools of pale aquamarine when she became confused.

This had him wonder... how would they respond in a moment of passion? An explosion of colors? All rolled into one? Maybe an ice blue... with a flash of fire to follow?

Whoa... where did that come from? You've got enough going on in your life right now without thinking of diving into a new relationship.

Startled at how quickly these thoughts had entered his mind, he shoved his hands in his pockets, his gaze traveling anywhere but at her. Since his mind was taking him to a place he had no business thinking about, it was time to get back to the matter at hand.

Rocking back on his heels, he cleared his throat. "Right now, I'm more concerned about those boxes you left out on the sidewalk. I don't know where you're planning on taking them, but was that a smart thing to do?"

Panic flashing across her face, Jessie sent a quick glance towards the door. Then, she slowly shook her head. "No one is going to take them. This is Blossom Falls. Things like that don't happen here."

He shrugged. "Okay, if you say so."

She stared him down, her response short and to the point. "Yes, I say so. Since I've lived the majority of my life in this town, I should know. People here are honest. They always have your back."

And there you have it… another flash of deep sapphire, aimed right at you.

He nodded. "In the same graduating class as Robin Miller, I was informed. Yes, I also know you grew up here. Along with a few other things."

Uneasy, she studied him. She wasn't sure she liked the smug look on his face. As if he knew something she didn't.

Exactly how much information had Crystal shared with him? Since she sometimes tended to be on the dramatic side, this becoming even more prevalent while she was pregnant, Jessie wouldn't be the least bit surprised if she had made her out to be more desperate than she already was.

Her brow furrowing in concern, she searched Max's face. "What exactly did Crystal have to say about me?"

A smile twitched his lips. "*Hmm…* let's see… only that your name is Jessie and you live in the city. She didn't share what city, but my first guess would be Chicago. Or maybe even New York." He shook his head. "No, I'm going to stick with Chicago."

He shook his head. "I can see it all so clearly. Small town girl seeking more to life, leaves behind her past and the girl she was to pursue a career in the big city."

When she didn't respond, her mouth falling open in disbelief, he grew uneasy.

Maybe you went a little too far with what you said?

He swiftly dug his hat and gloves out of his pocket and after pulling the hat down over his ears, he put on the gloves. Rubbing his hands together, he glanced over at her. "So, are you going to just stand there? Don't you have a delivery to make? Why don't you start out by telling me where the boxes are supposed to go."

Her eyes now even a darker shade of sapphire blue, her

response came out through gritted teeth. "I'm perfectly capable of handling this on my own, so why don't you just strut your way back to your car and leave me be."

And she meant this. She didn't need his help. No, what she wanted was for him to leave. Then she wouldn't have to listen to any more of his opinions.

Maybe, just maybe, he was right about what he said. When she was younger, yes, she had been okay with who she was. But it was when she was in high school, she realized her only hope in shedding her small-town-girl image was to leave behind the life she had become so comfortable with and move to a large city. There she would be able to make a new start, find a name for herself.

She'd prove to everyone in Blossom Falls there was so much more to the shy and quiet Carter sister. And for a while, it looked as though this was really going to happen.

But for some reason, during the past year or so, the climb to the top no longer seemed so important. Her job had taken over her life, leaving her on the constant edge of exhaustion. And even though she was making good money, her twenty-four-seven work schedule left her with no time to enjoy the perks she was now able to afford.

The drive to become the best?

To prove yourself?

Poof... it had slowly disappeared.

But it was this latest development at the firm that was her final wake-up call. Being asked to leave had her spiraling right back to her high school days. When she was sentenced to serve a detention for something she didn't do.

What was even more distressing? She had no desire to fight back. Not for her job, or her innocence.

You. Just. Don't. Care.

"Hey, wake up... are you dreaming, or what?"

At the sound of Max's voice, she glanced over at him. He had pushed back his sleeve and was pointing to his watch.

This was a reminder she'd promised Crystal the cakes would be delivered by eight. And if she didn't get moving, this wasn't going to happen.

Horrified at the angry tears that were beginning to build in her eyes and not sure why they were there, she turned her back to him. Yanking open the freezer door, she began removing the cake boxes, two at a time, almost tossing them on the counter.

After she grabbed the last two from the freezer, she gave the door an extra hard slam, this vibrating with a loud bang through the tension hovering between them.

Quickly swiping away any chance of tears, she glanced over to see Max was still there... watching her.

He warily raised an eyebrow. "Okay... so, now what?"

And there went her last hope. Evidently, he wasn't planning on leaving.

She tossed her keys to him. "My SUV is parked right out front. It's silver. You can start with the boxes that are already outside. Just load them in the trunk. But, again... you are in no way obligated to do this. I'll be more than fine if you want to leave."

Holding onto the keys he'd just barely snatched out of the air before they hit him in the chest, he peered more closely at her.

He groaned. "Jessie..."

Close to her breaking point, she'd already decided she was going to ignore him. Angrily swiping away another tear, she stacked five boxes on top of each other, picked them up and headed for the door.

Not a good move.

She should have known better than to take so many boxes at once. Their glossy finish had them sliding around, sending the top two slipping to one side. Even with her frantic attempt to right them, she knew she was in trouble.

Nope, she didn't have a chance.

And if the cakes hit the floor?

They would be ruined.

She tried to bargain with them out loud. *"Oh, nooooo, please don't fall. Please, no…"*

Curiously watching this play out before him, it wasn't until the boxes were on the verge of plummeting to the floor, Max came to life and grabbed them out of the air just in time.

Her shoulders slumped in relief, Jessie closed her eyes. She was waiting. Surely, he wasn't going to pass up the chance to make some kind of comment.

Yeah, you can't imagine him not having something to say about this.

But there was only silence.

Finally sneaking a glance over at him, her words came out in a mumble. "Thank you."

He moved closer. "Pardon me? What did you say? Was that actually a thank you I just heard?"

She groaned, closing her eyes. Was he ever going to give her a break? What did he want? A long and heartfelt apology? A comment on how wonderful he was?

Suddenly, she was too tired to care. She only wanted this day to be over. So, she could crawl into bed and go to sleep.

Maybe for a week.

Or at least until you get back to yourself, take on the world like you planned.

She opened her eyes and looking right into his, she gave him the biggest, brightest smile she could. "Yes, it was. I thank you from the bottom of my heart. Is that better?"

When he nodded, a big smile on his face, she jerked her chin towards the keys in his hand. "Now, since you have the keys, why don't you go first?"

He grinned again. "Yes, ma'am."

Frowning in response, she followed him out the door.

This nice guy act of his?

He didn't fool her one bit.

CHAPTER 7

Don't let the fear of striking out
Keep you from trying to hit that home run.
~ Anonymously Yours

After loading the last box in Jessie's SUV, Max waited for her to lock up the shop.

He couldn't believe how hard it was snowing. He'd also swear the wind must be blowing straight from the North Pole, sending the wind chill into single digits.

Pulling his collar up against the stinging snow, he was beginning to wonder why he still hanging around when he could be back in his nice, warm hotel room. A safe haven of sorts, with no one to pounce on every word that came out of his mouth.

Yeah, granted your accommodations aren't what you would choose, but they're looking pretty darn good to you right now.

Since Jessie had left Crystal's house in such a hurry she had forgotten her gloves. So, her fingers now almost completely numb, it was a real struggle to lock the door to the shop.

The wind blowing her hair in her face—yes, she'd also

forgotten her hat—she finally ran over to where Max was waiting by her SUV. Jamming her hands in her pockets, she tried to give him a smile.

Unfortunately, with her teeth chattering, this came out in more of a grimace. "Okay, we're done. All of the boxes are in my SUV. So, now I only have to deliver them to the community center and everyone will be happy. At least, I hope so. With Susan, the woman in charge, you never know."

She watched, puzzled, as Max opened the passenger door and began to get into SUV.

"Wait... what are you... I mean... what do you think you're doing?"

Sinking into the seat, he peered out at her from inside the SUV. "You have no gloves and no hat. It's snowing harder than before and I swear, it's even colder, So, I'm going to be the gentleman I was raised to be and help you deliver these cakes. You can drop me off by my car when we're done." He started to close the door. "*And please...* don't argue with me. I can see you're freezing. I don't want to be the one responsible for you getting sick."

He watched as she battled within herself over what to do before she finally gave another one of the huffy sighs he was becoming so familiar with. Marching over to the driver's side, she got in, slamming the door to let him know just how mad she was with this new development.

He held out his gloves. For a brief moment, she didn't move. Then after mumbling what he was pretty sure was a thank you, she slipped them on and started the SUV. From that point on, she didn't say a single word as they drove through town.

That is, until she came to a long... *a very long* ... stop at the crosswalk. This was even though there wasn't a soul in sight.

She shot a quick glance over at him. "Satisfied?"

But Max wasn't even paying attention.

He was busy checking out the interior of her SUV. A high-end model, it had every possible gadget available.

For some odd reason, this was a big disappointment to him. When it came to designer brands, he wasn't much of a fan.

So, why was he wearing a North Face jacket? His sister had given it to him last year for Christmas. And he had to admit, it did keep him warm.

But now, realizing they had come to a stop, he glanced over at Jessie to see she was staring at him, eyebrows raised.

He cleared his throat. "Sorry, did you say something?"

"No, forget it." Giving another one of those sighs of hers, she stepped on the gas hard enough to send them skidding through the crosswalk.

Now, Jessie knew she was acting like a child. Especially since she'd probably still be loading the boxes in her SUV if he hadn't been there to help. And he did give her his gloves to wear.

A designer brand, by the way. Coach, according to the label.

But there was something about him... and she couldn't put her finger on it... that had her ready to fight him, no matter what he did.

His voice filtered through her thoughts. "Nice SUV. An awful lot of gadgets, though. Do you really have a need for all of this?"

She briefly closed her eyes. And there you have it... the perfect example of why she was on the defensive, quick to feel so irritated.

Again? He didn't know her. So, he had no right to judge her.

Presumption of innocence... or innocent until proven guilty. Any way you want to say it.

Managing not to sigh, she sent him a long look. "I'll admit I like the comfort. And the convenience. And sometimes, you do what you need to do in order to fit in."

She paused, almost surprised by what she said.

Is this what you really believe? Fit in? This is what you want?

He was shaking his head. "Fit in, huh? To what, exactly? And what is it you do, that it's so important to fit in?"

Her mouth open, she was staring at him. That he had practically read her thoughts concerned her.

And hey... he should talk, decked out in his designer jacket and fancy hiking boots. He wasn't even hiking. Unless walking through town was his idea of exercise.

Pressing her lips together, she decided not to give him an answer. With the little she'd learned about him so far, his response would be too hard for her to top.

And, did it really matter? Because once they delivered the cakes and she drove him back to his car, she'd probably never see him again.

So... why bother?

When Jessie didn't answer, Max wondered if the issue of 'fitting in' could be the cause of her cranky mood.

Unbeknownst to her, he studied her as she drove.

Still windblown, her hair was a rich shade of warm amber, drops of melting snow sparkling like glitter in the curls and waves that fell to her shoulders. He found he was suddenly gripping the strap of the seatbelt, the temptation to reach over and run his fingers through the wispy strands framing her face, hitting him harder than it should.

He'd noticed she wasn't wearing much make-up. This was more than okay with him. He had found once his status as a pro-baseball player had risen, his popularity with women also sky-rocketed. But most of these women were heavy on the clothes and make-up in an effort to keep up a photo perfect image whenever they were with him. He began to suspect the photos were more important than him.

After all, he wasn't stupid. Not when they started showing up everywhere — Twitter, Instagram, Facebook, you name it... He hated that kind of self promotion.

He'd never been into any social media hype before and he had no desire to start now. The only time he really welcomed this type of publicity was when the request came from a true fan. Or it involved some kind of charity.

Actually, he was beginning to hate photos as a whole. He didn't even want to count the number of times he had to delete the photos that popped up, portraying him as this man around town.

He was not, and he would swear on this, a man who wanted people to think he liked to party the nights away, a woman on each arm.

But back to his assessment of Jessie. One of the first things he'd noticed about her was she was tall, her head coming right at his shoulder. With his six-foot-three-inch frame, this meant he didn't have to bend way down in order to look into her face.

Or into her eyes...

Yes, again... her eyes. He was still having a hard time trying not to think about how easily he got caught up in their blueness.

He glanced over at her.

She was studying him. And, his eyes meeting hers, once again, he was pulled right in.

She was the first to look away. And if he wasn't mistaken, even in the dim interior of the SUV, she was blushing.

A smile slowly worked its way across his face.

Really? Hmm...

Jessie pulled up to the front entrance of the Community Center. She stared down at the steering wheel, suddenly unable to remember why she was even there. Or what she was supposed to do next. Something that had been happening ever since she had first set eyes on Max.

One minute she hated him, wishing he would just go away. Then he would say or do something that got her so flustered, like letting her wear his gloves. Then she couldn't even think straight. This had her switching gears, trying to think of something to convince him to stay.

She couldn't actually be attracted to him, could she?

You just met him... and you really don't like him, so, how could this be possible?

She had no idea. Up until now, she had pretty much screwed up every relationship she was in, so she wasn't one to ask.

She took a deep breath. She was here to deliver the cakes and this is what she was going to do.

After she got out of the SUV, she glanced over at him. "Well, this is the place. Stay here until I make sure someone is there to open the door for us."

As soon as someone answered Jessie's knock, he unloaded some of the boxes and handed them to her. Then he grabbed more for himself and followed her into the building.

He almost ran right into her when she came to an abrupt stop and leaned over to whisper in his ear. "Just to warn you, I see Robin Miller is here. And I can tell by everyone's stressed-out expressions, she is on a roll and not to be messed with."

After she sent a quick glance around the room, she leaned in again to whisper. "I don't see Susan. Maybe she didn't want to deal with Robin, so she left."

He grinned. "Hey, she doesn't scare me. I can take on Robin any day."

Rolling her eyes, Jessie shook her head. "You think so, huh? We'll see about that."

What Max said wasn't entirely true. Robin did scare him. A lot. A woman who prided herself on being the first to know everything, it was obvious she also liked to be in charge.

And from his experience, this always resulted in a good deal of drama.

So, his plan was to ignore her. But he soon found this was easier said than done.

As soon as Robin saw them, she came rushing over, nearly shoving Jessie aside in order to get to Max. Barely giving him enough time to set the boxes on the table, she grabbed his arm and dragged him across the room. She pointed at a huge box filled to the top with tangled strings of lights.

At the same time, the words came flying out of her mouth so
fast, he found it almost impossible to understand what she was
trying to tell him.

"Oh... my... gosh... You can't possibly know how glad I am to
see you. You're like our long-awaited hero, destined to fix this
mess of lighting we've been left with." She sent a quick wave
over at Jessie, who was watching them. "I'm sure Jess won't
mind. There are plenty of people here to help her bring in the
cakes."

Still clinging to his arm, she gazed up at him. "Just to fore-
warn you, I always make it a point to get better acquainted with
anyone new in town. Especially someone as handsome as you
are."

A flirty smile on her face, she batted her eyelashes. "You're
like a breath of fresh air. And from what I've been able to find
out, it looks like you're also a man who has a lot of interesting
stories to tell. And I can't wait to hear them."

Glancing over at Jessie, he stifled a groan when he saw she
was glaring in his direction. Hoping her expression was aimed
more at Robin than him, he sent her a smile.

She responded with a toss of her head before she turned and
headed for the door.

Oh, geeez...

He turned to Robin. "I'm sorry, I'd really like to help you, but
I promised Jessie I'd help her unload the boxes. Since we both
have other plans, our plan is to make a quick exit once the boxes
are all accounted for."

He glanced around the room, zeroing in on a man who was
walking aimlessly around the room, a disoriented look on his
face.

Ah... he looks like a man who could use something to do.

He pointed him out to Robin. "What about that guy? I bet
he'd be able to help you."

Robin gave a very unladylike snort. "Milton? I sincerely
doubt he'd be of any help. Instead, he'd probably wind up re-

designing the whole batch, turning the whole process into some kind of experiment."

When Milton glanced over in their direction, Max gestured for him to join them. Once he reached them, Max reached out to shake his hand. "Hey, nice to meet you. I'm Max."

He nodded over at Robin, who was shaking her head, clearly unhappy with this blip in her plans. "Robin could really use your help with these lights. They're being very temperamental. Do you think you can take a look?"

When Milton began searching through the box, ignoring Robin's frustrated expression, Max began backing away. "Okay, then. It looks like Milton is on the job, so you're set. I'll see you around."

He headed for the door, almost colliding with Jessie as she came back inside, carrying a load of boxes.

Too many boxes.

He frowned, shaking his head. Evidently, she hadn't learned her lesson about how many boxes one person should carry in order to avoid a catastrophe. Because once again, he was just in time to save the top two boxes from hitting the floor.

But this time Jessie didn't thank him, instead sailing right past him to set the boxes on the table.

She turned to him. "Well, this was the last of them. Let me tell one of the committee women the cakes are all here. Then we can leave."

With that she was gone.

His hands jammed his hands in his pockets and the expression on his face not a happy one, he could only wait.

Jessie was about to pull out of the parking lot when her phone rang. The screen on the dashboard showed the call was from Crystal.

She glanced over at Max. "I have to answer this. Otherwise I wouldn't put it past her to get in her car and drive over here to make sure everything is all right."

He nodded. "Sure, I understand."

Jessie hit answer. "Hey, you called at the right time. We just delivered the cakes, everyone is happy and I should be home in about fifteen minutes."

Crystal's sigh traveled through the SUV, loud and clear. "Thank goodness. And again, thank you. I owe you, big time."

Jessie laughed.

Max glanced over at her in surprise. Believe it or not, this was the first time he'd really heard her laugh.

He smiled. He liked it.

Crystal's voice came over the speaker again. "But, wait a minute... what did you mean, we delivered the cakes? Who is we?"

Jessie sent Max a look of panic. This actually made him chuckle as he jumped in to answer Crystal. "She meant me... Max. Remember we met earlier? Before I forget, I want you to know I am now one of your newest fans. I wish I had taken a cake of each flavor, the one I chose was that good."

Crystal laughed. "You can stop by anytime and I'll give you as many as you want. In fact, how would you like to come over for dinner Saturday night? I make a mean lasagna. Ask, Jessie, she'll confirm this."

His first instinct to refuse Crystal's invitation, Max looked over just in time to see Jessie shaking her head. Then, a look of complete horror on her face, she groaned, plopping her forehead down on the steering wheel.

This made him a little mad.

Seriously? Does she really think you're that awful?

And this had him changing his mind. "I accept with pleasure. As long as you can promise Jessie will also be there. I know she is also very appreciative of my help and would want to be a part of this dinner."

There was a short silence before Crystal responded. "*Hmm...*

how interesting you should say this. But, yes… I will make sure she's there."

She laughed. "So, it's a date? Seven-thirty, Saturday night? And, hey… if there is a girlfriend or fiancée… or even a wife in your life, they're also invited."

His gaze going to Jessie, he hesitated when he saw she had become very still. It was only when she reluctantly lifted her head to look over at him, he sent her a smile before he responded to Crystal. "Nope, none of those apply. It will be only me. And lasagna is one of my favorites, by the way. Saturday night, seven-thirty."

Jessie swiftly took over the conversation. "Okay, Crystal… I'll be home in a little bit. Bye." She turned off her phone and without a word began driving to where Max had parked his car.

He was the first to break the silence. "Jessie, if you'd rather I didn't come on Saturday, I won't. But I'll let you in on a little secret… I'm really not that bad once you get to know me."

She sighed. "No, it's fine. If Crystal were to find out you cancelled because I don't want you there, she would never—and I mean *never*—let me hear the end of it. She's been trying to marry me off for the past five years."

She groaned. "Not that this is what she's trying to do with you and me. But I've learned, as far as she's concerned, any man in a hundred-mile radius is fair game. Doesn't matter what they look like or how smart they are…the main criteria is they're available and preferably male."

She shook her head. "Again, I'm not insinuating you fall into this group. Of course, this isn't what I meant. It's only that I need to be careful. I don't want to wind up with some—"

He cut her off. "Okay, I get it. There's no need to explain any further." He pointed at the only other car in sight. "And there's my car, so you can drop me off right here."

After she came to a stop, she waited for him to get out of her SUV. But this didn't happen. This filled her with a sudden guilt, wondering if maybe an apology was in order. After all, she hadn't been very nice to him since they got into her SUV.

More like the whole evening, you mean.

Instead she remained silent, watching as he pulled on his gloves before he smiled over at her. "Well, it's been fun." He suddenly chuckled, shaking his head. "And I guess it's not going to end here, is it? Who would've thought?"

When her only response was a faint smile, he opened the door. Then he abruptly turned back to her. "I don't know what happened. Or what's causing you to be on the defensive, especially with me. But if you need someone to talk to, I'm here for you. You can ask any of my friends, or even my family, and they'll tell you, I'm good at listening. I don't judge, and I won't tell you what to do. I'll just listen."

He smiled over at her. "I've found sometimes this is all it takes for someone to realize they can figure it out on their own." Then he reached over to brush his knuckles along the side of her jaw, smiling when this sent a tremor sailing through her, to then travel right back through him.

Did this mean there was some kind of chemistry between them?

You'd have to say there was. Definitely…

This had him forgetting all about the cold, the snow, and basically everything else. Pulled in by the different shades of blues swirling in her eyes, he moved closer, his voice coming out so unbelievably husky. "It's going to be okay. I promise."

For a brief moment, he hesitated. Then he opened the door, turning once more to give her a wink. "Until Saturday night, then. I'm looking forward to it."

She watched as he cleared his car of snow, turning to wave before he drove away. But even after his car had disappeared into a blur of white, she still didn't move. She didn't understand.

"It's going to be okay. I promise."

How could he be so sure of this? And was he going to stick around to make this happen?

It was a good thing she didn't have far to go. With the state she was in, it was a miracle she remembered her way home.

In fact, she almost missed the street Crystal lived on.

She blamed this on the long day she'd had. It had nothing to do with Max.

Absolutely not.

Closing the door as quietly as she could, Jessie silently made her way down the hall.

She peeked into the living room.

Jackson was still asleep on the sofa. It appeared Crystal was also asleep, her head resting back against the cushions, her eyes closed.

She decided to let them be, turning to leave.

Crystal's amused voice put a halt to that. "Hey, not so fast. Don't think you can run off to bed without telling me what went on between you and Max tonight."

Jessie sighed.

Oh boy, here we go…

After making a big production out of hanging up her coat and taking off her boots, she shrugged. "Nothing went on. He came into the shop thinking it was you who was there. I'm pretty sure I was the last person he wanted to see. Then he offered to help me load the cakes in my SUV. And even though I told him I didn't need his help, he insisted on going with me to help deliver them to the community center."

She frowned. "Robin was there. Why didn't you remind me how annoying and pushy she is? She practically pounced on Max as soon as we walked in, dragging him over to help her fix lights or something."

Crystal was smiling. "*Hmm…* I see. And this made you mad?"

Jessie glared at her. "No, it did not."

Crystal nodded. "*Ah…* and did he help her?"

"No, surprisingly, he didn't. He told her he had somewhere else to go. As a matter of fact, he told her we both had to leave. So, she wasn't very happy. I hope she didn't take it out on Milton, since Max roped him in to help her instead."

Crystal laughed out loud at this. "Milton has had this thing for Robin for years."

She nodded over at Jessi's surprised expression. "Yes, he told me this a while back. But he wants to wait until her divorce has been final for at least a year before he even asks her out. I think they might be perfect for each other." She sent Jessie a thoughtful look. "So, what did you think of Max? He seems like such a nice guy."

Jessie gave a frustrated sigh. "I don't know what to think of him. If anything, he made me angry most of the time, always on guard. I'm pretty sure I argued with everything he said."

She shook her head. "He seems so pretentious, a know-it-all type of guy. And believe me, I've dealt with enough of his kind to know the outcome is never good."

She frowned over at Crystal. "And then you go and invite him over for dinner? Why? You don't even know that much about him. He could be dangerous. Or a dangerous criminal, on the run."

Crystal started to laugh. "A criminal? You really think so?"

Shaking her head, Jessie dragged her hand through her hair. "Okay, so maybe not. But if this is your way of trying to fix us up, *please*... don't. A man is not what I need right now."

Yeah, what you need is a job. And a reason to believe in yourself again. Because the last man you got involved with stole both those things away from you.

Crystal smoothed the quilt down over her stomach, a nonchalant smile on her face. "I liked him. He seemed so genuine. I also thought he might need a friend or two, feeling sort of alone right now. Moving from California to Cleveland can't be a very easy move. Especially, with the way our weather has been lately."

She glanced over at the window, where the snow was already starting to pile up on the sill. She sighed. "It's going to be a long winter if this keeps up. Especially with a newborn in tow."

After a silence, she sent a tentative glance over at Jessie, her words hesitant. "You do know sometimes your emotions can play tricks on you, don't you? Hate can very easily get confused with love?"

Jessie laughed, wondering why it came out sounding so unconvincing. Almost to the point she wasn't even sure if she believed what she was about to say. "Crissy... I am not in love with the guy. Or even attracted to him. Far from it. I know you like him, but I can tell you right now, he's not the one for me. "

A wistful smile settled on her face. "When I fall in love, I want to be happy. Not on edge all of the time, worrying about what we're going to disagree on next. And most of all, I don't want any surprises."

"*Hmm*... I see." Nodding, Crystal didn't have any response beyond that.

For a while, they were both silent. It was the sudden shifting of the logs in the fireplace, sending sparks shooting up the chimney that had Jessie coming to her feet.

She gave a huge yawn. "I really need to go to bed, and so do you. It's been a long day." She glanced over at Jackson, who hadn't stirred the entire time they had been talking. "Do you want me to get Jackson up to bed?"

Crystal shook her head. "No, I'll take care of him." She glanced out the window again. "Gosh, it's still snowing. I hope Max makes it home all right." She smiled at Jessie. "Goodnight. I'll see you in the morning."

Jessie didn't sleep well. And she put the blame for this on Crystal and her comment about Max driving in the snow.

It's only normal to be worried about him. You'd be worried about anyone in the same situation.

Right?

But as she tossed and turned, long after she knew he was already home, safe and sound, she knew she was fooling herself.

She didn't understand, why couldn't she stop thinking about him? After all. starting up a relationship with him, or anyone else, wasn't in her plans right now.

But then something he'd said or did popped up in her mind, and she was off, reliving another moment of the time they spent together.

So, it was almost dawn before she finally fell into an exhausted sleep.

To dream of coffeecakes and icicles in the snow.

CHAPTER 8

*I*t was Saturday night, the delicious aroma of homemade lasagna wafting through the house.

After helping Marilyn at Crystal's Coffee Cakes all day, too busy to even take a break, Jessie was starving.

She glanced around the bedroom. It was a mess.

Clothes were thrown across the bed and even more were draped over the chair. And, for the life of her, she still couldn't decide what to wear.

She groaned, and slowly sinking down on the edge of the bed, she put her head down in her hands.

What are you doing? The guy isn't coming only to see you. It will just be the four of you, Jackson included. It's a dinner shared with friends. Nothing more.

So, there was no reason to be so concerned about what she was going to wear. Max probably wasn't even going to notice what she had on. And even if he did? Once he had a taste of Crystal's lasagna, there was a pretty good chance he'd forget about her altogether.

She smiled. She couldn't think of a single person who didn't claim Crystal's lasagna was by far the best they'd ever had.

The sound of the timer going off downstairs, signaling the

lasagna was ready to be taken out of the over, was a reminder she should already be dressed and downstairs, helping Crystal with the dinner preparations. Even though Crystal had refused her earlier offer of help. She claimed Jessie had already done enough, filling in for her at the shop today. And with the long nap she had been able to take, she was now well rested and ready to go.

Now Jessie only needed to quit fooling around and get dressed. Max was due to arrive in about twenty minutes.

Just throw on a pair of jeans and an old sweatshirt... let him think you couldn't care less about what he thinks.

She sighed. No matter how much she tried to convince herself otherwise, she knew this wasn't what she was going to do. She began rummaging through the clothes on the chair, finally pulling out a v-neck sweater dress.

Even though this was a dress she had owned for years, it was still one of her favorites. A deep royal blue, with the hem hitting right below the knees, she always felt good when she wore it. The simple lines of the dress could fit almost any occasion depending on the choice of accessories.

Tonight, she was going to pair it with her black boots. And for jewelry? She'd keep it simple with her silver hoop earrings and sterling silver necklace.

The necklace, with its hand-made angel charm, had been a gift from Crystal when she passed the bar. She had told Jessie to think of it as her own special guardian angel to watch over her as she began her career as a lawyer.

Jessie gave the angel a stern look.

It seems you're shirking your duties right now, no?

After she slipped into the dress, she glanced over at the clock on the nightstand. She had about fourteen minutes to pull herself together. Maybe a little make-up was in order?

Unless it was a special occasion, she usually didn't wear make-up. But for tonight, she figured why not? Starting with a little eyeshadow and a touch of mascara.

With two minutes to spare, she was on her way down the stairs.

Max was nervous.

Really nervous.

He was a pacing back and forth, constantly checking the time and second-guessing himself kind of nervous.

That this behavior had been with him since Jessie dropped him off at his car the other night, was something he was trying not to think about.

Yeah… good luck with that.

How could this be? It had only been two nights, yet it felt more like two weeks.

So, as you can imagine, he was having a hard time trying to figure out what his problem was.

He could only remember his nerves kicking in like this when he played in his first world series game. When he was at bat, with the game on the line. The kind of pressure he wouldn't wish on anyone.

But right now? He had gone above and beyond this, his anxiety level now high up on the scale, possibly all the way to the top.

She's just another girl.

And therein lies the problem. For some reason, his mind wasn't buying this.

She was far from just another girl.

He couldn't quite put his finger on it, only that there was something different with the way he felt when he was with her.

Again, he was going to blame this on those amazing eyes of hers. Even just the thought of them sent his heart hitching in his chest, a sudden longing to be with her coming over him.

How many times in the past couple of days had he wished he'd gone with his gut feeling and kissed her before he left her SUV?

Yeah, aren't you the one who's always spouting off about trusting your instincts? This has worked for you in the past, so why not go with it?

He glanced down at his watch. He didn't have time for this. He needed to stop thinking so much and get ready. Running his hand slowly down over his beard, he stared at his reflection in the mirror. The beard was a new look for him, and he wasn't quite sure about it yet. He thought it would be easier to take care of, but he'd swear he spent all of his time trimming and combing the darn thing. He didn't want to fall into that scruffy lumberjack kind of look.

He slipped into his new light grey sports jacket, his reflection finally smiling back at him.

Yeah, you're looking good, buddy. You made the right choice with this one.

His choice of black Henley, jeans and boots, all of which he'd treated himself earlier today, had him feeling pretty good. If nothing else, his choice of apparel was right on the mark.

Stuffing his wallet in his jeans pocket and grabbing his keys, he checked the time.

It was six-forty-five.

Good... he had time. There was a stop he wanted to make.

Whistling, he headed for the door.

CHAPTER 9

Some people are worth melting for.
~ Unknown

Jessie surveyed the messy room in front of her, shaking her head. "Jackson, it looks like a hurricane went through here."

Lounging on the huge pile of pillows he'd carefully arranged on the floor, and completely zoned into the show he was watching on TV, he didn't hear her.

So, she clapped her hands, loud enough to get his attention. "Come on… help me clean up a little. Then you need to go upstairs and change your shirt. I swear, it looks like you've been rolling around in it."

He grinned up at her before making a big production of rolling across the floor. After he came to his feet and gave a long stretch, he threw the pillows back on the sofa and turned off the TV.

He brought his shirt up to his nose and sniffed it. "Do I really need to change? It doesn't smell. So, it can't be too dirty."

Jessie pointed towards the stairs. "Just go put on a clean shirt. Because our guest will be here any minute. "

He started up the stairs, but stopped halfway to give his opinion of how he felt about her request. "Okay, okay... I'll find another shirt. But it's not going to matter. I bet this guy won't even care what kind of shirt I'm wearing."

He stopped again to peer down at her. "Is this your boyfriend?"

She made a face at him. "No, heaven forbid. Your mom is the one who invited him. She thinks he's lonely and needs a home cooked meal."

"She's too trusting." This was muttered under her breath as she arranged the magazines on the end table.

Jackson peered over the railing at her. "What did you say?"

Sending him a smile, she waved him up the stairs. "Nothing, just go get dressed."

Jackson thought about this for a moment before he shrugged and went leaping up the stairs.

Jessie folded up the quilt, turned off the TV and headed for the kitchen. She found Crystal taking the pan of lasagna out of the oven. After she set the pan on the counter, she glanced over at Jessie.

She smiled. "*Wow...* you look really nice. I've always loved that dress on you. It makes your eyes even more blue."

She glanced over at the clock on the microwave. "Everything is ready. Max should be here any minute now."

As if on cue, the doorbell rang.

Crystal smiled. "Good, he's right on time. But then, I'm not surprised."

When Jessie didn't move, she tilted her head, an amused look on her face. "Well, are you going to answer the door? I would, but I'm pretty sure you'll get there a lot faster than I ever could."

Jessie couldn't move. It was almost as though she was anchored to the floor.

And she had absolutely no explanation, only that for some odd and unexplained reason, she felt as if everything was about to change when she opened the door and found Max standing there.

"Jessie? Are you all right?" Crystal grinned. "I don't think you're in any danger. He's not going to bite. Now, if he tries to kiss you... that's a different story. One that could turn out to be a very dangerous, but memorable, I'd think... especially for you."

This was enough to galvanize Jessie into action. Glancing over at Crystal, she stuck out her tongue. "Stop it... that's not even funny. A kiss is the last thing I want from him. Remember? I told you, he's not my type."

Crystal shrugged. "Whatever. Now, go answer the door. Let the guy in already."

Jessie opened the door to find she was face to face with a huge poinsettia plant.

The plant suddenly shifting to one side, Max gave her a tentative smile.

"Hi."

And, in what felt like a blink of an eye, something gave way inside of her. The frustration and anger he usually brought out in her?

This had completely disappeared.

It was as though she was seeing him for the first time.

So, as you can imagine, the smile she gave him was just as tentative. If not a little bewildered.

"Hi?"

His gaze slowly traveling over her, Max was silent. It was only after he lifted his head, he spoke. "Wow, Jess... you look amazing. Your eyes, the dress, everything. But then, I swear a man could get lost in your eyes. In fact, I believe I already have."

Yes, if you could look into her eyes forever, you'd be happy man.

This sudden revelation actually had him taking a step back, wondering why what he'd said had come to him so easily and so fast.

But what was even more confusing? There would be so many other things he would like to say.

And all of it would be good.

In a heartbeat, you would. You'd only need a sign…

He smiled. "Do you think I could come inside? I was told by the woman in the florist shop, cold weather isn't good for a poinsettia plant."

After she stepped aside so he could enter, he set the poinsettia down on the hall table. There it appeared even larger, towering over everything.

He glanced over at her, a wry smile on his face. "Maybe this is a case of bigger isn't always better. It certainly didn't look this so huge in the florist shop."

Then he smiled. "*Ah…* but this should make up for my blunder." He reached inside his jacket and pulling out a single rose, he held it out to her. "This is for you."

The rose was a beautiful shade of lavender.

Surprised at the unusual color, she smiled as she took it from him "Thank you. I've ever seen a rose this color before."

He cleared his throat. "This particular color was suggested to me by the florist. I've never thought much about flowers, their colors, or what they signify. But thanks to the extensive knowledge of the florist, I now know there are specific rules you should follow when giving the gift of flowers."

He smiled. "And when I told her the message I wanted to share with you, she suggested a lavender rose."

Twenty minutes ago, he certainly hadn't thought he'd still be listening to a lecture on flowers from the woman manning the florist shop. But because of the wintery weather, it was a slow night. So, the woman had been more than eager to share her knowledge of the language of flowers.

A smile slowly curving her lips, Jessie searched his face. "And what message are you trying to send?"

He smiled, shaking his head. "*Ah…* I'll let you look up that information yourself. Maybe later, after I leave."

The sound of someone coming down the stairs, they watched as Jackson came bursting into the room.

He took one look at Max and came to a dead stop. His mouth falling open and his eyes going wide, he stared at him for a good ten seconds.

His gaze finally swiveled over to Jessie, a huge smile spread across his face. "Why didn't anyone let me know this was the guy my mom invited to dinner?"

He then turned to Max. "I can't believe you're standing right here in my house. You..." Here he stopped to shake his head. "Max Kirby... *the* Max Kirby. *Wow*... this is amazing. The guys on the team are going to go nuts when they hear about this."

His hands in his pockets, Max glanced over at Jessie before he nervously cleared his throat. "I believe Jackson – this is your name, right? Jackson?"

At Jackson's grinning nod, he looked over at Jessie. "I think what Jackson is trying to say, he may have recognized me and –"

Jackson interrupted him. "Recognized you? Anyone who knows anything about baseball would know who you are the minute they saw you. Why, you're the super star of professional baseball,"

He grinned over at Jessie. "Aunt Jessie, he is one of the greatest baseball players around. Cleveland signed him only about a week ago for a ton of money."

Max was shaking his head. At the same time, he was trying to avoid eye contact with Jessie. He was also beginning to think he may have made the mistake of not letting her know who he was.

But, in his defense?

It hadn't come up. Since they had spent most of their time arguing, any talk of baseball or any other details of their lives simply hadn't found a place in their conversation.

He wasn't the type of guy who threw this kind of information around, whether it be to impress people, or brag about what he did for a living. He liked to keep things as low key as he could. As far as he was concerned, playing ball was a job just like any other job. As he had been quick to remind his family and friends many times, as the choice of careers go, he got lucky.

He shot a quick glance over at Jessie.

She was staring at him, the expression on her face almost identical to Jackson's.

But there was one difference... there was no big smile on hers.

Nope, there wasn't even a trace of one.

Uh, oh... it looks like you're going to have a lot of explaining to do.

He moved closer, searching her face to see if he could get an idea of what she was thinking. While she was searching his just as intently.

She shook her head. "I don't know what to say, why—"

He moved even closer. "Jessie, I'm sorry I didn't tell you, but let's face it, we never even got to discussing that part of our lives. Trust me, it's just a job. Like any other job."

An eyebrow raised, she nodded. Very slowly she did this. "A job, you say. Just like any other job. Come on... seriously? I don't think so..."

He groaned. "Believe me, this is exactly the way I see it. I have to prove myself like everyone else. And what Jackson said? I'm no superstar."

He directed his next comment to Jackson. "There are no super powers involved. I work very hard at what I do, and have been, ever since I was even younger than you are now. I never take any of my success for granted. And I never will."

Crystal's voice came from behind them. "Well, I think it's wonderful. Now I know why you seemed so familiar. Your face has been all over the sports pages."

She smiled. "From what I've read, everyone is very excited you decided on Cleveland, Max. The thinking is you're what the team needs, you'll bring a spark to the organization."

She put her arm around Jackson. "I know this guy was

thrilled when you accepted Cleveland's offer. He's one of their biggest fans."

Glancing from Max's worried face, to Jessie's one of uncertainty, she gave Jackson a gentle push towards the kitchen. "Come on... I need you to help me carry the food into the dining room before everything gets cold. You can ask Max all the questions you want once we're seated."

After Crystal and Jackson left the room, Max glanced over at Jessie.

She was frowning down at the rose in her hand.

He groaned. At the same time, he reached over and cupped her chin in his hand, lifting her face to his. "Jessie, look at me."

He had to briefly close his eyes at the confusion he could see in hers, so many shades of blue, swirling in a turmoil.

"Jessie, you aren't mad, are you?"

She hesitated, searching his face. Then she slowly shook her head. "I... I don't know. I don't know what to think."

He moved closer to her. "I wasn't trying to hide anything from you. Honest, if you think about it, the subject of what I did for a living never even came up."

Shoving his hands in his jean's pockets, he sighed. "I've found as soon as people find out who I am, they treat me differently. And this was something I didn't want from you. It also didn't help you were so angry, your trust at a low. I'd be willing to bet, if I had told you I was a professional baseball player, you would've accused me of trying to impress you."

His head tilted, he started to smile. "Admit it... this is exactly what would've happened."

He watched a faint smile flicker across her face before she sighed. "I can't believe I'm saying this, but you're probably right."

Relieved, he smiled. *"Hmm... I'm probably right?"*

She sighed, giving him an actual smile this time. "Ok, I'll admit it... you're right. But don't let it go to your head."

He smiled, watching as she brought the rose to her lips, the smile still there. Then she realized what she was doing, and dropping her hand to her side, color filled her cheeks.

She glanced towards the kitchen, her voice suddenly coming out all breathless. "We better go join them. Otherwise, Crystal will send Jackson to check up on us. But be prepared. He's probably going crazy right now, thinking about the millions of questions he wants to ask. He is most inquisitive child I know. And he loves baseball with a passion. But, don't feel obligated to answer them if you'd rather not."

Relieved the whole subject of him being a professional baseball player was now out in the open, and Jessie appeared to be okay with this, Max was willing to answer any question Jackson threw at him. He reached over to tuck a strand of her hair behind her ear. "I don't mind. I do a lot of mentoring with kids his age because I can remember what it was like for me during that time of my life."

He searched her face, still worried. "So, we're okay, then?"

At her nod, as if it was the most natural thing in the world, he reached for her hand. "Good, let's go put Jackson out of his misery."

He grinned. "To tell you the truth, I'm looking forward to his questions. You wouldn't believe some of the things kids ask me."

Max set his napkin next to his plate. "Crystal, everything was amazing. Again, I want to thank you for inviting me."

He sent a grin over to Jessie. "I'm glad I didn't turn down your invitation."

After gulping down the rest of his milk, Jackson looked over at Max, a serious expression on his face. "Aunt Jessie said my mom invited you over for dinner because you're lonely and hadn't had a good meal in a long time. I don't understand... why?"

Embarrassed, Jessie groaned. "Jackson... that is not what I said. I said your mom invited him over for a home cooked meal. There's a big difference. And by lonely, I meant Max is new in town. Moving to a new city is always hard at first. You miss your friends and family."

She glanced over at Max. "Please disregard what he said. Those were his words, not mine."

Pushing his broccoli around on his plate, trying to make it look like he ate more than he should have, Jackson was frowning. "But what about the other guys on the team? Aren't you all friends?"

At Max's nod, he continued. "Our team has already made a pact we're going to stick together, play on the same team. And, we're not going to wait until we're old, like thirty or something, to finally go pro. Is that what happened to you?"

He searched Max's face, waiting for an answer.

Max laughed. "Hey, are you saying I'm old?" Running his hand through his hair, he glanced over at Jessie and Crystal. "And here I was, thinking I have a few good years of playing ball still ahead of me. I know I won't be playing forever, but I try not to think about that. My plan is to enjoy it while I can." He shrugged. "Because who knows what the future holds?"

Here he hesitated, glancing over at Jessie. There was a slight smile on his face. "In the meantime, I've been hoping someone would come along and give me something more pleasurable to think about than baseball."

Jackson gave a loud snort, bringing a warning glance from Crystal. "Jackson... where are your manners?"

He grinned. "Sorry."

Then his face scrunched up in disgust, he turned to Max. "*Yuck*... you mean girls, don't you?" He vigorously shook his head, sending his hair flying. "I want nothing to do with girls. Not now and not when I'm older. They only cause trouble."

Max laughed. "You're right, they do cause trouble. But as you get older, you'll find it's a whole different kind of trouble and you'll change your mind."

He glanced over at Jessie, who had now begun to clear the table. Coming to his feet, he reached for the stack of plates she was holding. "Let me help you." He gestured to Jackson. "I think you and I should be doing the cleaning up here. Your mom and Jessie have already done more than their share. Especially since, between the two of us, we ate most of the lasagna."

Her head propped up on her hand and her eyes half closed, Crystal sighed. "Oh, Max... you are such a sweetheart. I don't understand... why haven't you been snapped up already?"

Ignoring the threatening look Jessie was sending her, she continued. "Or is this your choice? I imagine the life of a baseball player, with the constant travel and such a long season, is hard on a relationship, isn't it?"

She paused to think about this. "*Hmm*... you and Jessie are two of a kind. She feels the same about her career."

Now Jessie was frantically shaking her head. But Crystal just kept on talking. "I told Jessie, and the same goes for you, there is no reason you can't have both. Kids, too. If you really love someone, you make it work." She shrugged. "Look at me and Joe. Our life is far from easy. But I knew from the very beginning his commitment to the military was something he takes very seriously. And now, look at us. We have a baby coming, possibly any day now..."

Her voice trailing off, she gave a long sigh. "And it can't come soon enough for me."

Max glanced over at Jessie. Her head down and frantically gathering up the glasses and silverware, she was trying to completely avoid him.

He cleared his throat. "Jessie, I don't believe you ever told me exactly what it is you do for a living. Or where this even all takes place. Thanks to all of Jackson's questions, I feel like you know almost my whole life story. So, it's only fair, I know more about you."

She mumbled something before she headed for the kitchen, the lasagna dish in her hands.

He glanced over at Crystal.

She smiled. "She's a lawyer, in Chicago. I'm not surprised she didn't tell you. I think I bring it up more than she does. But only because I'm so proud of her. Believe it or not, growing up, she was always so quiet and shy."

Crystals comment had Max staring into space as he tried to remember what he'd said to Jessie the other night.

"I can see it all so clearly. Small town girl seeking more to life, leaves her past behind to pursue a career in the big city."

Running his hand through his hair, he groaned. This wasn't good, more than enough to make him feel like an insensitive jerk. Even though, give him credit, he'd called it right... he did pick Chicago.

"Max?" Crystal was studying him, eyebrows raised.

He sent her a big smile. *"Wow... Chicago, huh? Nice city. My mom was hoping I'd play there. It's where she grew up. So, Jessie came here to spend Christmas with you?"*

Crystal sent a quick glance towards the kitchen, where they could both hear Jessie and Jackson arguing about something. A wry smile on her face, she patted her stomach. "I'm embarrassed to admit I called her in one of my weaker moments, shamelessly begging her to come home to help out in the shop. I honestly didn't think she'd say yes. Or show up so soon."

She leaned closer to him, her words coming out in an exaggerated whisper. "I think there's something else going on... either with work or Chad."

This immediately had Max's attention.

Chad? Who's Chad? A boyfriend?

He didn't like the sound of this... "Chad?"

After another furtive glance towards the kitchen, Crystal

nodded. "Chad is this guy she was dating. But from what she's told me about him, he doesn't sound like a very nice person. A lawyer in the same firm, I get the impression he's not too smart and is using Jessie. They've worked on quite a few cases together. Or should I say, Jessie's worked on the cases, with Chad showing up at the last minute to take most of the credit."

As if she suddenly realized she may have said too much—not that this had ever stopped her before—she gave Max a big smile. "But knowing Jess, when she's ready, she'll tell me what's going on. Speaking of ready, I hope you saved room for dessert? And it's not even cake. I made an apple pie."

The words had no sooner left her mouth when Jackson came into the room, a big grin on his face and proudly carrying the pie. Jessie was right behind him with plates and silverware.

After she set them down on the table, she pulled a phone out of her pocket and handed it to Crystal. "Here, you left this in the kitchen again. I thought you might want to check your messages, since it looks like someone has been trying to call you. More than once, it seems."

Looking down at the phone, Crystal groaned. "It's Susan. We're working together on the Coats and Toys for Tots drive and I swear, she calls me at least a half-dozen times a day. She can turn the smallest problem into a huge disaster in nothing flat."

She set the phone on the table.

It started ringing again.

She sighed. "I better answer it." She nodded over at Jessie as she began leaving the room. "Go ahead and start serving the pie. I'll try to keep this short."

After she was gone, Jackson looked over at Max. "I want a big piece. How about you?"

Max laughed. "I'm embarrassed to say the same since it looks so good. But I'm going to be polite and take whatever size slice Jessie cuts for me."

Both he and Jackson were arguing about the size of the slices Jessie was cutting when Crystal came back into the room.

She looked like she was on the verge of tears. This was confirmed by the single tear slipped down her cheek.

Jessie set the knife down on the table and made her way over to her. "What's wrong? What happened?"

Crystal slowly sank into one of the dining room chairs, "Someone broke into the community center storage room and stole everything we've collected for the coats and toys drive. They left nothing behind. Susan said even the rolls of wrapping paper and this big box of ribbons and bows are gone. I don't know what we're going to do. We were so careful to make sure every gift was tagged so we'd know who it was for. We only had a handful more to finish the list."

Wearily running her hand through her hair, she sighed. "I don't understand how someone was able to do this without being seen. It just doesn't seem possible."

After swiping away another tear she slowly came to her feet. "Susan is at the community center. I told her I'd meet her there. Maybe we'll be able to find some kind of clues. Or at least come up with a plan of what to do next. But I don't know how we're going to fix this. We have not even a week to replace what we lost. And no money left in the budget."

Jessie gently pushed her back into the chair. "You're not going anywhere. Remember? You're supposed to be taking it easy. I'll go."

The pie momentarily forgotten, Jackson jumped up out of his chair. "I'm coming with you, Aunt Jessie. I'm a really good detective. I'll take that big magnifying glass dad gave me and check every inch of the place for evidence."

Jessie gave him a hug. "I'm sure you're a great detective, but I think it would be best if you stayed home with your mom."

Max nodded. "Jackson, your Aunt Jessie is right. You need to keep your mom company. I'll go with your aunt. And don't worry, I'll be sure to fill you in when we get back."

Jessie looked over at Max. "You don't have to come with me. I'll be—"

He interrupted her. "Yes, I'm well aware of your reluctance to accept my help. But, whether you like it or not, I'm coming with you."

His direct gaze letting her know he wasn't going to back down, he watched as her eyes began to darken with anger.

Jessie was angry, all right.

Just when you were beginning to think he wasn't all that bad, now he pulls this macho act on you? You don't need his help.

Sensing the tension between them, Crystal spoke up. "Max that would be wonderful. I'll feel so much better knowing Jessie isn't alone and in the dark this late at night." She smiled over at Jackson. "While they're gone, you and I will have a piece of pie with an even bigger scoop of ice cream."

Jessie was staring at her, incredulous.

What? So late at night?

She checked her watch, then shook her head. It wasn't even eight-thirty. This was Blossom Falls they were talking about.

The worst crime you can imagine right now would be someone throwing a snowball at you. Or singing Christmas carols too loud.

Max had left the room. When he returned, he had his coat on, and was holding Jessie's. Still angry, she reached for it, but he shook his head. "Let me help you."

He winked over at Jackson. "My parents drilled it into me, you should always be the perfect gentleman. Even though you aren't too keen on girls right now, remember to keep this in mind. It will pay off later in life."

He leaned closer to Jessie, his whisper for her alone. "Even when the girl is angry at you."

He opened the door and taking her arm, he smiled over at Crystal. "Again, thanks for dinner."

He pointed his finger at Jackson. "And don't even think of eating my slice of pie. Unless you don't want to go to the ballpark with me sometime soon. Just to check it out."

Jackson's grin went from ear to ear. "Don't worry. I'll guard your pie with my life."

CHAPTER 10

For Jessie and Max, both the walk to his car and drive to the community center was a silent one.

Yes, she was still a little miffed he'd invited himself to go with her.

He really should have asked.

And, yes... she knew she was acting childish about this. But for some reason, once again and through no fault of his own, he managed to get her all worked up. And this just kept happening. There was just something about him that had her on guard and ready to attack, every single second she was with him.

Max had decided to take his cue from her, even though he didn't know what she was so mad about. In his mind, offering to go with her was a no brainer... the right thing to do.

But to be honest? There was also one other very important reason he'd volunteered his company so quickly.

He wanted to spend some time with her.

Alone.

Not with Crystal.

Not with Jackson.

Nope...

Just with Jessie...

It wasn't that he had anything against Crystal or Jackson. No, he liked them. They were great people. But they weren't who he wanted to be with.

You want to be with Jessie.

Was this really too much to ask?

He wanted be able to share a real conversation with her, get to know her better. And he had foolishly thought he'd be able to get a start on this during their drive to the community center.

He shook his head... Seriously? What was he getting himself into? He wasn't one to turn down a challenge, but she had to be the most confusing woman he'd ever met.

Yeah, her mood changes so fast, you can't keep up.

So, hoping for one of these change of moods, this one for the better, he remained silent.

By the time they pulled into the community center parking lot, sure enough, Jessie was consumed with guilt. As they began walking towards the main entrance, she came to a stop and put her hand on his arm. "Wait... before we go in and get caught up in all of the drama, I want to thank you for coming with me. I'm sure there's a million other things you'd rather be doing right now. But just to warn you, Susan, along a few of the other women, can be very dramatic and –"

Before she could finish what she wanted to say, he grabbed hold of her hand and pulled her up against him.

"Jessie..." This coming in a long groan, for one very brief moment his eyes held hers. Then, his hand gently cradling the back of her head, he captured her mouth in a deep, searching kiss.

At first, she remained rigid in his arms. But this was only because the kiss was unexpected.

So unexpected.

Then her hands slowly moving up to grip his arms, she fell right into the kiss. And she fell hard... returning his kiss with a passion beyond what she'd ever experienced before.

Max would be the first to tell you this kiss was just as much of a surprise to him as it was to her. It definitely wasn't what he'd planned.

Definitely not...

He'd thought about it, yeah... more than once. Half a dozen times, or maybe even more. Starting from the moment she greeted him tonight at the front door. Her eyes, the dress, the first genuine smile she gave him... they had hit him head on, flooding his mind, awakening his senses. To the point, she was all he could see.

And now? Giving her this kiss felt like the smartest move he'd ever made.

His lips slowing, he went on to press a trail of feathery kisses across her face before resting his forehead against hers.

His voice was husky, barely a whisper. "You have no idea how much I've been wanting to do this. In fact—" His mouth swooped down to capture hers again. But this time the kiss was sweet, gentle... but more than enough to have them both completely falling back into the moment.

His lips slowly brushing over hers once more, he leaned back, his gaze roaming over her face.

Faced with her dazed expression, his eyes searched hers. "Are you all right?"

Jessie didn't know.

Was she?

No, she'd have to say she was pretty much in shock.

Definitely...

She buried her face against the hard wall of his chest. She needed a little time, that's all. A little time to catch her breath, calm her heart. If only to convince herself this had really happened.

And the most important thing of all?

You hadn't tried to stop him... nor did you want to...

"Jessie... honey? Are you okay?"

She lifted her face to his, nodding when she saw the concerned look on his face.

His body relaxed against her in one long sigh of relief. "Thank goodness. I thought I might have moved too fast, too soon." Then his mouth brushing over hers, he chuckled.

She leaned back, her look searching. "You find kissing me amusing?"

He pressed a kiss to her forehead. "Oh, no... absolutely not. But it's all so crazy. If someone had told me a few days ago I'd be kissing you, I would've told them they were out of their mind. Not after the rocky beginning we had. We certainly didn't hit it off, did we?"

His smile had her smiling, too. She shook her head. "This was because you were so pretentious... and bossy. Two of the traits I find most offensive in a man."

He tightened his hold on her. "Jessie, one look in your beautiful eyes and you had me so I couldn't even think straight. I went right into denial." He shook his head. "I put on my tough guy act, trying to convince myself I didn't need anyone. Most of all, I didn't need you."

He shook his head. "But, that didn't work. You had already found a place in my mind and you've been there ever since."

Thinking he'd be more than happy to stay right where they were, maybe share another kiss, it was a big gust of wind, sending a shower of snow down from the trees, that had Max reaching for her hand instead. "Come on, I don't want this to end with us freezing to death in the parking lot of the Blossom Community Center. With our luck, Susan would be the one to find us. Or worse yet, it could be Robin."

"*Yoooooo Hoooooo...* Whoever you are... wait for me."

This coming from behind them, they turned to see someone was headed in their direction, frantically waving to get their attention.

Jessie groaned. "Oh no, speak of the devil, it's Robin." She glanced over at Max. "Just to warn you, Susan and Robin disagree on everything. And this has been going on *forever.* Which means there will be a lot of drama, and emotions will be riding high. So, if you want to leave, go. I won't hold it against you."

Shaking his head, he chuckled. "And leave you here to face the two of them alone? No way. Lawyer or not, I'm sure you can use my help."

She shot him a startled glance. "How did you—"

Dressed all in black, Robin came to an abrupt halt right next to them. She shrieked, grabbing onto Max's arm when she almost slipped on an icy spot on the sidewalk.

Her other hand going to her heart, her sigh was annoyed when she saw Jessie. "Oh, it's you again."

Still holding Max's arm, she moved closer, her words coming out in dramatic little gasps. "I am *so*... *so*... out of breath... but I heard... the missing gifts... so I came right away..." Leaning against him, she took in a huge breath, her words tumbling out in one long exhale. "I had to see for myself what's going on."

Batting her eyelashes up at him, she gave a little giggle. "Am I lucky, or what? Because, here you are again."

Jessie wanted to scream.

Who does this anymore? Flirt like this?

She watched as Robin tightened her grip on his arm, dragging him along with her. Talking non-stop, her shrill laugh echoed loudly through the silence of the night

Max sent her a desperate look over his shoulder. Unable to hide her smile, she gave him a little wave.

She couldn't wait until she could remind him of what he said. You know, how he'd thought she needed his help?

Hmm... maybe it was the other way around?

CHAPTER 11

Sometimes on the way to a dream,
you get lost.
But then you get lucky and find a better one.
~ Anonymously Yours

When Max, Jessie and Robin walked into the community room, they found Susan talking on her phone. Pacing back and forth, waving her hands for emphasis, at first she didn't realize they were there.

She finally glanced over in their direction, and abruptly ended the call. After adjusting her glasses, she peered over at them.

Her gaze fell on Robin. She frowned.

She glanced over at Jessie, her look accusing. "Where is Crystal? When I told her what happened, she told me she would be the one to come here."

Then, jerking her head over at Robin, she gave a huffy sigh. "I certainly didn't expect to see her."

Jessie sighed. "You know Robin always has a way of finding out what's going on. And *come on...* give Crystal a break. She's supposed to be taking it easy. This is the very reason I came back home… to keep everyone in this town from taking advantage of her."

"I am not taking advantage of her. She offered." In an attempt to hide her guilt, Susan's attention shifted to Max. "I'm sorry, should I know you? Have we met?"

Max held out his hand. "Hi, Susan. We did meet the other night when I helped Jessie deliver the cakes for your luncheon. But at the time, you had a lot going on. So, I can understand how you might not remember me. I'm Max, a friend of Jessie's."

Robin loudly cleared her throat. "But why not tell her who you *really* are… tell her your last name, Max." She paused dramatically, a smug smile on her face as she glanced from Jessie to Max. "It's Max Kirby, right?"

Briefly closing his eyes, Max nodded. "Why, yes… you're right, Robin. Max Kirby, that's me."

Susan was watching them, a puzzled expression on her face. "Robin, what is your problem? Does it really matter what his last name is? We're not big on formality here."

Crossing her arms over her ample chest, shifting them so she appeared even more endowed than she was, Robin smiled sweetly at Max before she glanced over at Susan. "Susan, I can't believe you didn't recognize him. Why, as soon as he walked in the room the other night, I realized who he was. He's the talk around town right now… Max Kirby, the newest member of Cleveland's baseball team. He's been all over the news and there are photos and articles about him in just about every newspaper."

She sent another smile over at Max. "Even though I couldn't find any info on your marital status. But going by your age, I assume you're married. So, you must bring your wife to Blossom Falls. I don't know a woman who comes here and doesn't rave about our quaint little town and all it has to offer."

Max shrugged, a closed expression on his face. He had absolutely no plans of playing twenty questions with this woman.

There was a reason Robin couldn't find anything about him. His personal life was one thing he liked to keep private.

And he intended it to stay this way.

Hoping Robin took his silence as a sign the subject was closed, he turned his attention back to Susan. "Have you called the police?"

She shook her head. "No, I wanted to wait until I talked to some of our other members," here she glared over at Robin, "members I can trust will not go blabbing around town before we know more details. I'm also hoping maybe one of them might have an explanation for what happened."

She sighed. "For some reason, I just can't get it out of my head whoever did this must be desperate. More than we could possibly understand."

Surprised by her comment, Max slowly nodded. "*Hmm...* you may be right."

The sudden sound of a siren and screeching tires had Susan and Jessie glancing suspiciously over at Robin.

She shrugged. "That must be Bobby. I'm sorry, but I felt it was my duty to notify the police. Theft of any kind is a criminal action and not something to be taken lightly."

Jessie had moved to stand next to Max, leaning in close enough to whisper in his ear. "Robin has had a crush on Captain Gunn ever since high school. She calls him for every little thing. I'm surprised he puts up with her."

A smile twitching his lips, Max also spoke in a whisper. "You're serious... Captain Gunn?"

She nodded. "Yes, very serious. Bobby's last name is Gunn, but with two n's. I've known him since grade school and it has always been his dream to be, as he puts it, a man of the law. Even back then, his nickname was The Captain. Right after graduation, he sailed through all of the required training with flying colors. As one of the three men on the force, he takes his job very seriously. But between you and me, I think he watches way too many crime shows on TV."

She sighed. "You're about to see Blossom Falls at its' finest. So, be prepared for a real show."

A man came charging into the room, his hand ready and hovering over his gun holster. A large man, with the tight fit of his uniform, close to bursting at the seams, he was obviously a man who also loved his food.

He barked out his greeting, this coming out loud enough to make everyone cringe. "Captain Gunn, here."

After quickly scanning the room, he zeroed in on Susan, tipping his hat in her direction. "Don't worry, Mrs. Hillard, ma'am... I have someone securing the outside premises as I speak."

Robin had covered the distance between them in a flash, clinging to his arm. "Oh Bobby, it's so terrible what happened. Someone took all of the Christmas gifts we were planning to distribute to the less fortunate families in the city."

She dabbed at invisible tears. "And now we have nothing. We're crushed. Our dreams of providing even a tiny ray of hope and joy in the life of others, hoping to make their Christmas a happy one, has been snatched away from us. And so brutally and senselessly at that."

He held up his hands and jumped back from her, nearly tripping over his own feet in the process. "Gosh darn it, Robin, how many times have I told you it's not a good idea to come running at a man with a gun. I'm on duty here, my mind zoned in on the situation at hand and you never know how I might react."

He gave her a stern look. "And again, may I remind you? It's Captain Gunn. I go by Bobby only when I'm off duty."

Completely ignoring Robin's pouting expression, he pulled a small notebook and pen out of his pocket, directing his attention to Susan. "Now Mrs. Hillard, ma'am, can you tell me what you know about the break-in."

Susan gave an exasperated sigh. "Oh, for crying out loud... call me Susan. There's not much to tell. Mainly because I wasn't here when it happened. I stopped by to drop off a box of donations that was turned in today and walked in to find everything gone. This would be the gifts and all the trimmings, nothing else. Not that there is anything else to take. But, I believe whoever did this must have known the center wasn't in use tonight."

His hand stroking his chin, Bobby gazed slowly around the room. "*Hmm...* this indicates the culprit or possibly culprits, as in more than one, must be familiar with the premises." Having said this, Bobby began writing furiously in his notebook, his brows furrowed in concentration.

There was the sound of more sirens, followed by car doors slamming. Two more of Blossom Falls finest came rushing into the room.

Without looking up from his writing, Bobby yelled out his orders. "I want the two of you to do a thorough search of the area, dusting for prints, the works. You know the drill."

Max was watching all of this, totally fascinated.

Observing this, Jessie leaned in to whisper in his ear again. "Robin was the star of our drama club in high school. To this day, she claims she gave up her dream of becoming an actress to stay here in Blossom Falls. For the past five years or so, she has been campaigning to bring the theater here instead. Her goal is to raise enough money to build a theater right in town. So, don't be surprised if she comes at you asking for a contribution."

She hesitated before her next words came out rather sharply. "Or she might go after your wife, try to get her involved."

Yes, Max had been in her SUV, and sitting right next to her, when she heard him tell Crystal he wasn't in a relationship. But the evasive manner in which he just responded to Robin's comment about a wife made her wonder if he hadn't been all that truthful. But how could he have kissed her so passionately if he was already married? Maybe her first impression of him had been right?

You've seen enough of those magazines in the grocery store checkout lines to know what goes on in the life of the rich and famous.

Let's face it... she was a lawyer.

She needed more facts.

Max groaned. He was torn.

He had received Jessie's message loud and clear. Which meant he needed to set her straight.

He did not have a wife. And never had.

That she would even think this after he had told Crystal he was pretty much free as a bird, well... this had him a little angry.

Did she really believe he'd give her a kiss like he had if he was married? Heck, he was still reeling over how that kiss made him feel. A kiss like he'd never before given to anyone, it had surprised even him.

But this wasn't the time or place to tell her this. Right now, there was something more important occupying his attention. This would be Bobby's reaction now that he realized Jessie was in the room.

After Bobby had slapped his notebook shut and stuffed both it and his pen into his back pocket, he headed over to where the two officers were huddled in the corner of the room, embroiled in a heated argument about who was responsible for what job.

This was when he saw Jessie. His eyes widening in surprise, he came to an abrupt halt. Slowly removing his hat, a smile crept across his face.

Unfortunately, Max wasn't the only one who witnessed this.

Robin did, too.

She was across the room and hanging onto Bobby's arm in less than five seconds flat. She pointed over at Max. "Bobby... *ooops*... sorry, Captain Gunn... look who wandered into our humble little town? I've been trying to convince him this would be a wonderful place to settle down while he's here."

Tearing his gaze away from Jessie, Bobby peered over at Max. A confused expression on his face, he frowned as he turned back to Jessie. "Did you go and get married on us? If I'm not mistaken, I recall Crystal saying you were pretty serious about some guy in Chicago."

His mouth suddenly dropping open, he stared at Max in disbelief. Then after he slapped his hat back on his head, he held out his hand. "Let me be the first to congratulate you on your marriage. You're getting a real prize here. I've been sweet on Jessie for years, but I guess she sees something in you I couldn't give her. I think she got spoiled living the big city life."

He shook his head. "But I made it clear to her a long time ago, that's not the life for me."

Horrified, Jessie was shaking her head. "*Oh, no, no...*"

Max reached over to press his fingers to her lips. "It's okay, sweetheart. I told you we'd probably have a hard time keeping this quiet. We'll just have to change our plans a little."

Closing her eyes, she gave a frustrated sigh. "But—"

He put his arm around her, cutting her off with the kiss he pressed to her mouth. "I told you, hon... it's going to be fine."

Shoving his hands in his pockets and rocking on his heels, Bobby jerked his head over at Max. "*Sooo...* in order to ease my mind Jessie is in good hands, what is it you do? Are you a lawyer, too?"

Robin, who was eying Max and Jessie suspiciously, completely confused with this new development, reached over to give Bobby's arm a good swat. "Bobby Gunn, you are a moron. You watch baseball, don't you? This is the new player Cleveland signed. He's supposed to be the best player in the whole country."

This had Max shaking his head.

The whole country? You don't think so. You're flattered, for sure. But again, you're no superman.

He glanced over at Bobby. Eyes narrowed, he was frowning.

Max cleared his throat. "That's quite an exaggeration, Robin. I'm average at most, with a few good days thrown in every once in a while. My only hope is I'll be able to help Cleveland's team as much as they believe I can."

Robin sent Max a bright smile. "This is a perfect example of why I decided to dedicate my life to bring more culture into this town. No one keeps up with anything... I swear, it's like we're living in our own private little bubble, oblivious to everything around us."

Uncomfortable under Bobby's heated gaze, Max gestured over to where Susan was now talking to the other two officers. "We should probably check to see if they've found anything."

This galvanized Bobby into action. Adjusting his pants and then giving a good tug to his hat, he gave Max a brisk nod. "Yes, you know what they say, the more time that passes, the less chance you have to solve the case." He turned on his heel and went striding over to Susan.

Robin glared at both Max and Jessie. She shook her head. "You two don't fool me one bit." This said, she whirled around and headed towards the door. Where she made sure to slam it as hard as she could after making her exit.

Max looked at Jessie, his eyebrows raised. "Wow... what the heck just went on here?" He shook his head. "I feel like every time I turn around, I'm hit with another display of dramatics. Is this what living in a small town does to a person?"

Jessie shrugged. "What can I say? This is what happens when everyone knows everything about everyone else."

She frowned. "Heaven forbid you make a mistake. The only thing you can do at that point is to beat it out of town."

He studied her, a smile twitching his lips. "A mistake? Is this what happened to you? What did you do that you had to leave town? Something scandalous?"

She gave an irritated sigh, avoiding his gaze. "Nothing, I did nothing." She nervously peered over to where Susan, Bobby and the two officers were talking. "We should join them. Find out what's going on."

He grabbed hold of her arm as she began to walk away.

"Wait... before you go, like I told Crystal the other night, I'm not married. But I didn't want to tell Robin this. I didn't feel it was any of her business, okay?"

She shook her head. But he saw the flicker of a smile cross her face before she went over to join Susan and Bobby.

Not even bothering to hide his smile, he slowly sauntered after her.

Adjusting his hat, Bobby's expression was one of complete seriousness as he spoke. "Well, it seems whoever did this was very careful to hide their tracks. We found a candy cane on the floor, but don't know if this is something we should look into. After all, at this time of year, candy canes are all over the place."

He shook his head. "So, we'll have to move to Plan B. Start checking around town, try to find out if anyone has seen or heard something."

Hooking his thumbs on his belt, he gave a slow nod. "Yep, for now, there's really nothing we can do but go home and get a good night's sleep. In the meantime, maybe we'll get lucky and the morning will bring in some new evidence."

Susan was wringing her hands. "But what will we do? How are we ever going to replace all the gifts we've lost?"

Max cleared his throat. "Maybe I can help? I'm sure I can rustle up some help."

"Rustle up some help? Where are you from, cowboy? Out west?" After finishing off his comment with a loud snorting laugh, Bobby gazed around at everyone, surprised no one appeared to share his joke. Turning red with embarrassment, he mumbled under his breath. "Come on, people... rustling isn't something we do here in Blossom Falls."

Max ignored this, turning to Susan. "Do you have a master list of the gifts? If so, make a copy and email it to Crystal. I'll see what I can do." He nodded over at Bobby. "Hopefully, by the time I get the list, you'll have solved this case. But if not, we'll fix this."

He reached for Jessie's hand and headed for the door. "Come

on, sweetheart. I haven't been able to spend any time alone with you all day."

He winked. "You still owe me dessert, if I'm not mistaken."

Max was surprised Jessie hadn't commented to what he said. But at the same time, he knew darn well her silence was only temporary.

Sure enough, once the door to the community center closed behind them, she yanked her hand away. She began walking so fast, he almost had to run to keep up with her.

He was trying not to smile. "*Hmm...* why do I get the impression you're mad at me?"

She whirled around and her hands going to her hips, she glared at him. Her eyes were every shade of blue possible, every emotion coming through, big time. "Max Kirby, what were you thinking? By tomorrow it's going to be all around town you and I are either engaged or married. And, what exactly did you mean about that comment I still owe you dessert?"

She raised her face to the sky, letting out a long groan. "I'm sure they all took it the wrong way."

He had no intention of letting her know his behavior had been in response to Bobby's obvious crush on her. That he became so jealous and felt such a sudden possessiveness had almost blown him away.

Come on... you're jealous of Bobby? Are you nuts?

So, since he wasn't quite sure how to answer her, he went with the same response that had worked earlier. He pulled her into his arms and captured her mouth in another kiss, one even more passionate than the last.

This was when he realized a kiss was no longer just a kiss. With Jessie, it was different. Everything had changed with that first kiss they'd shared. Like a drug, a sweet, intoxicating drug... he'd swear her kisses had now become almost as necessary as breathing.

It was only when she pushed her hands against his chest, he released his hold. For a few long moments, breathing hard, they stared at each other.

He was the first to make a move. Briefly closing his eyes, he shook his head. "Again, I'm sorry. But it just seemed right." He shrugged. "I like kissing you. But if you want, I'll stop"

Slowly running her hand through her hair, she shook her head. "I... you... you've got me so I can't even think straight. This is just so... I don't know... sudden? Why, I don't even know anything about you. And you don't know anything about me. I..."

She shook her head again.

She looked so serious, he smiled, pressing his finger to her lips. "*Shh...* you're thinking too much. And you haven't answered me... do you want me to stop?"

She didn't answer. Instead she began walking away from him, taking a shortcut through the snow-covered grass to where his car was parked.

He chuckled and catching up to her, he grabbed her hand. "Okay, with your silence I'm going to assume your answer is a no. So, how about I change things up a bit, slow it down?"

He shook his head. "Even though I can't guarantee—"

Whirling around, she came at him, sending him staggering backwards. Losing his balance, he hit the ground, with her landing on top of him. Before he could say a word, she framed his face in her hands and proceeded to give him a kiss that sent all doubt from his mind what her answer was.

When she finally lifted her head, she fell right into his smile.

His gaze roaming her face, he slowly shook his head. "*Whoa...* I wasn't expecting that."

At the worry beginning to swirl in her eyes, he reached up to frame her face in his hands. His whisper brushed across her face. "But, I liked it. I liked it a lot. You can give me an answer like that anytime, anywhere, honey."

She was smiling when, this time, he was the one to kiss her.

The sound of shouts and slamming car doors had her abruptly lifting her head before she gave a horrified cry. *"Oh, my God...* what if they see us?"

When she began to struggle against him, he wrapped his arms around her. *"Hey, hey, hey...* stay where you are. They aren't coming this way, so they won't see us. But if you start jumping around, we'll definitely attract their attention."

She closed her eyes. Her cheek resting against his chest, she could feel the beat of his heart, so steady, so strong. While hers was beating like it was running a marathon.

But this was understandable. After all, she was the one with a reputation at stake. If word got around town the police discovered them, wrapped up in each other's arms in a snowdrift, she'd never live it down.

And if she was forced to come up with an explanation for their behavior?

She wouldn't have one.

How could she, when she didn't even know herself why she appeared to have lost what little dignity or common sense she had?

His hand drifting slowly through her hair, Max cleared his throat. "Hey, it seems they're gone now. This means we can get up and out of this snow. A good amount has gone down my collar and it's darn cold."

This had her scrambling off of him. But before she could stand, he beat her to it, holding out his hand to pull her up with him. Retrieving her hat from where it had fallen in the snow, he handed it to her. He smiled. "It looks like you have glitter in your hair."

He grinned. "Snow glitter. If I didn't know better, I'd think you were an angel... a snow angel."

Her answer to this shot out on it's own accord. "Are you as complimentary with all of your girlfriends?"

As soon as she saw the confusion filling his eyes, she became flustered. Making a big production out of shaking the snow from her hat, she put it on. It was only after she pulled on her mittens, she glanced over at him.

He was studying her, a thoughtful look on his face. He shook his head.

And now she was on the defensive. She shrugged. "What?"

He moved closer. "Jessie, I'm more than happy to give out compliments to all the women I know. Because, you tell me, who doesn't like receiving a kind word now and then?"

All the women he knows? Was he kidding? There's a lesson to be learned here. He's not a one woman kind of man.

Wrapping her arms around herself, she began trudging through the snow towards his car. "It's late. We should probably get going."

Max checked his watch. It was not quite nine-thirty. She considered this late? *Hmm…*

But as he caught up to her, he decided not to say anything. In fact, he didn't say a word even after they were in the car. Or during the entire drive to Crystal's house.

Not that their drive was a long one. Even with the snow-covered streets, it was at the most, ten minutes. But with the silence like a wall between them, to Jessie it felt more like hours.

And Max?

For him, it felt even longer. This was because, once again, he was confused.

He didn't understand… couldn't she see he liked her? And after that kiss she gave him? He'd be willing to bet his entire collection of signed baseballs, and yes, this would be all thirty-three of them, give or take a few, she liked him, too.

But for him, like wasn't really enough to explain how he felt about her. Maybe this was the problem? He was moving too fast for her?

Or here's a thought… maybe you're just plain crazy? Or like your grandfather used to say, barking up the wrong tree?

Because what man would keep trying to win over a woman who kept pushing him away?

It shouldn't be this hard.

Nope, it should be simple.

Max pulled in the driveway and turned off the ignition. Resting his arms on the steering wheel, he glanced over at Jessie.

She was studying him, a worried look on her face.

Believe it or not, you should probably take this as a good sign. At least she didn't go vaulting out of the car in a rush to get away from you.

He smiled at the irony of this. He'd already come to the decision this wasn't going to happen. He wasn't leaving until she told him what was bothering her. Remember? Being a good listener really was one of his better qualities.

Watching as she absentmindedly traced the snowflake pattern on her mittens, he would have been very surprised to know she was trying to think of a way to ask him to stay. Her intuition was telling her if she didn't, there was a good chance she might never see him again.

The apple pie. Ask him if he wants to come in for the piece Jackson promised to save for him.

She turned to him, a tentative smile on her face. "It's…"

At the same time, he started to speak. "Jessie…"

He chuckled. "You go first."

She took in a deep breath. "I wanted to say, since it's not as late as I thought, and if you're still interested in a piece of Crystal's apple pie, you should probably come in. Otherwise, Jackson will gobble it up. As skinny as he is, I can't believe how much he eats."

A slow smile coming over his face, he nodded. "Sure, I'd like that. Maybe Susan sent Crystal the gift list. If she did, I can start asking around as early as tomorrow morning, get a start on replacing some of the gifts."

She hesitated, about to speak. Instead, she began pulling on her mittens.

He put his hand over hers. "Just say it."

She sighed. "I don't want you to feel obligated to help out with the gifts. For all we know, tomorrow morning we'll find out there was an uproar about nothing. Having seen the way things work in this town, I wouldn't be surprised if there was some kind of mis-communication. As my mom used to say, there are too many cooks in the kitchen."

He shook his head before he opened his car door. "It's okay, I feel like my life is in a good place right now and it's about time I started giving back."

Then he grinned. "I'm also hoping I might have a better chance of getting you to agree to a favor."

She watched as he jumped out of the car and came around to open her door. Knowing she was about to ask him what he meant, he chuckled. "Nope, no questions. We'll talk about it later. Right now my mind is focused on the apple pie you promised."

"Oh... and you, too." She felt the smile on his lips as he leaned in to kiss her cheek.

"You and homemade apple pie. These two things alone are enough to make me a very happy man."

CHAPTER 12

*W*hen Jessie and Max walked into the house, Jackson immediately jumped up from the sofa where he had been watching TV. He ran over to them, his words tripping over each other in his excitement. "What happened? Did you find the crooks? Did they leave any clues?"

Max shook his head. "No, unfortunately we didn't solve a darn thing. There were no clues or evidence to be found."

Jackson groaned, slapping his palm to his forehead. "You probably didn't look in the right places. I knew I should've gone with you."

Hanging up their coats, Jessie laughed. "No doubt you would have accomplished more than we did. I hope you saved that piece of apple pie for Max."

Crystal came into the room. "Not only did he save Max a piece, he also decided he wanted to wait until you came back so we could all eat dessert together."

Jackson sent Max a hopeful grin. "Maybe you can tell us more baseball stories?"

At Max's nod, he turned to Crystal. "You and Aunt Jessie go sit down in the living room. Max and I will take care of the pie and ice cream."

After Crystal and Jessie watched them disappear into the kitchen. Crystal was the first to speak. "Well? Tell me everything."

Fingering the angel charm on her necklace, Jessie shrugged. "Like Max said, nothing happened." She made a face. "Robin showed up. I don't know where she was coming from, but she was dressed all in black."

She shuddered. "With that poofed up hair of hers, she looked pretty scary. Somehow, she found out what happened and she called Bobby. He put on quite a show for Max. Both he and Robin did. Oh... and before I forget, Susan is going to send you a copy of the gift list. Max asked her to do this. He said he wants to help."

"*Hmm*... that's all good. And what a nice gesture on Max's part. But I'm more interested in what happened between the two of you?"

She sighed. "From what I can see, he's smitten by you."

Jessie laughed. "Smitten? Only you would use a word like that. And I disagree with you. I think he's a player... he knows what he needs to do in order to get what he wants."

Crystal frowned. "Jessie, come on... be fair. I have a feeling you really don't believe this. You've got to stop thinking every guy is like Chad. My intuition tells me Max is a keeper."

Jessie shot a quick glance over at the kitchen before she lowered her voice. "I don't think so. From what I've read..."

Crystal burst out laughing. "You've been checking him out? And yet you act like you want nothing to do with him." She was grinning. "And tell me... what exactly did you find when you were checking him out?"

Jessie put her finger to her lips, sending another glance over at the kitchen. "*Shh*... he's going to hear you."

Her voice was now down to a whisper. "The article said he recently broke it off with this woman who is now engaged to a guy who was on the same team Max played for in Minnesota. This tells me he's certainly not interested in starting up another relationship. No, I have a feeling he'd rather play the field for a while."

Crystal grinned. "But then again, you might be just what he needs." She peered closely at Jessie. "*Hmm*… what can we—"

Her words coming to an abrupt halt, she smiled over at Jackson and Max as they came into the room, Max was carrying a tray with cups and a coffee pot. Jackson's tray was loaded with the pieces of pie, almost unrecognizable under the huge scoops of ice cream piled on top.

Once the pie was passed around, Crystal sent a casual glance over at Max. "So, Max… what are your plans for Christmas? Do you spend it with your family? And where would this be?"

Setting his fork down on his plate, Max smiled over at her. "Before I answer that, let me say this is the best apple pie I've had in a long time. You should offer these in your shop. Now… as to where I grew up, this would be in Southern California. And out of my brothers and sisters, I'm now the furthest away from home. Since my parents are big on all the usual Christmas traditions, I'm hoping to get back there at least for a few days during the holidays." He grinned. "I know my mom would love Blossom Falls, because this is her kind of town. She complains every year about how commercial the holidays have become."

Crystal nodded. "It sounds like your mother and I could be good friends since I completely agree with her." She waved her fork at him. "Well, if you're around, you are more than welcome to spend Christmas with us. We're not fancy, but we also have our own fun traditions."

Max smiled. "Thank you for the invitation." He then glanced over at Jessie, a teasing glint in his eyes. "Now, I wonder… do you second this invitation?"

Not knowing quite how to answer this, she took the only way out she could… she smiled. Right before she shoved a huge chunk of pie in her mouth.

He nodded. "*Hmm*… I think I'll take that as a yes."

Jackson had finished his pie and after gulping down the rest of his milk, he plunked the glass down on the table. He gave Max a thumbs up. "*Yessss...* we need another man around here. It's not easy being the only one. I don't think I'm going to last until dad comes home in January."

Crystal shook her head. "Jackson, I think between me and Jessie, you have it pretty good. More than good, I'd say."

She smiled over at Max. "So, tell us about your family. How many brothers and sisters do you have?"

As he began filling Crystal in on his family, Jessie watched his face as he talked, his enthusiasm so contagious. At the same time, she was trying not to think about how she was getting so used to him being around.

He glanced over at her, the corner of his mouth lifting in one of those teasing smiles he was always so quick to give her. Even when he knew she was angry or didn't agree with what he said, bringing her to smile right back at him. Like she was now.

And then there was the gentle way he held her in his arms, the tenderness in his gaze right before he kissed her.

She closed her eyes, just thinking about this.

"Jessie?"

She blinked.

When she saw all eyes were on her, she jumped up from the sofa and began loading their dishes back on the tray. Avoiding any eye contact with Max, she headed for the kitchen.

After Max and Jackson helped Crystal get up from the sofa, she smiled over at Max. "While Jessie does that, I'll check my computer to see if Susan sent me the list."

She turned to Jackson. "And it's time for you to say good-night. You have an early hockey game tomorrow." She put her arm around him. "Come on, I'll go upstairs with you."

Max wandered into the kitchen just as Jessie closed the dishwasher. More like slammed. At least this is how it seemed to him. When she vigorously began wiping down the counter, flinging the towel around with such force it was almost frightening, he reached over and gently removed it from her hand.

He sighed.

"*Jess…*"

She leaned back against the counter and crossed her arms. After giving him a long searching look, she shook her head. This had him moving closer, his smile hesitant. "*Sooo…* are you going to tell me what's wrong? And please don't say nothing. Because I know this isn't true. I'm also smart enough to know it probably has something to do with me."

She took a deep breath. "What do you want from me?"

And now it was his turn to shake his head.

Reaching over to slowly pull her against him, he gave a sigh of relief when she almost, but not quite, melted against him.

His hands drifting down her back to hold her even closer, he pressed a gentle kiss to her forehead. His words were just as soft. "What do I want from you? I want to see you smile. I want you to talk to me, tell me everything about yourself. I want to know the real Jessie. Not the Jessie who is hiding who she is, what she's thinking."

His breath was a soft brush across her cheek, his voice almost a whisper. "I want the Jessie who threw herself at me, knocking me down in the snow so she could give me a kiss I haven't been able to stop thinking about."

When he felt her lips part in a smile, his voice dipped even lower. "This is what I want, Jessie. Everything that begins with you."

Jessie was lost. Seriously, this was *not* what she expected him to say.

Clutching the sleeves of his sweater, she didn't want to let go. But then it was more like she couldn't let go. His words had her weak in the knees, her heart beating faster than it had only moments ago.

Drawing in a deep breath, she lifted her face up to his.

His mouth brushed over hers, this time lingering a little longer. "Kiss me, Jessie. Kiss me like you did before."

Instead, she glanced sharply over at the door before she

abruptly pushed him away. Grabbing a dishtowel and a plate, she shoved them right at him.

"Here," she hissed, "start drying. Or at least, pretend that you are. Crystal's coming."

Bewildered, Max turned around to see Crystal walk into the kitchen.

A triumphant look on her face, she waved the papers she was holding. "Look what I have. But why am I surprised? I should've known Susan would send this right out."

Catching sight of Jessie's flustered state and Max's guilty smile, she stopped in her tracks. Slowly handing the papers to Max, she smiled over at Jessie. "I'm sorry. I hope I didn't interrupt anything? I wanted to get the list to Max before he left."

She frowned. "I forgot how big the list is, over six pages long. But, thinking back, I remember Susan telling me we received more requests this year than ever before."

She shook her head. "I sincerely hope whoever took all of those gifts had a really good reason for doing so."

She turned to leave. "And now I'm going to bed... for good, this time."

She grinned. "Thanks again, Max. And thanks for spending time with Jackson. I know how much he misses his dad."

He smiled. "My pleasure, he's a great kid."

Once she left the room, he tossed the papers on the table. Crossing his arms over his chest, he gazed thoughtfully over at Jessie.

She was busy folding the dishtowel. After she placed it on the counter, she glanced over to see he was studying her, his expression unreadable. She sent him a defensive glance. "What?"

He shook his head. "Would it have been that bad if your sister saw us kissing?"

She groaned, dragging her hands through her hair, "Trust me, you don't want to encourage her. Remember what I told you? She is never going to be happy until I find someone who she feels is good enough to marry me. And in case you haven't noticed, it's more than obvious she has decided you fit all of her requirements."

Closing her eyes, she groaned. "But of course, I don't—"

He moved quickly, pulling her into his arms before she could finish. "*Ah, Jess...* give her a break. This is what families do. Believe me, my sisters and mom are just as bad. But right now? I don't care what any of them think. I'm more interested in what you and I were—should I say discussing—before Crystal interrupted us. I believe you were just about to kiss me?"

A smile curved her lips. "You don't know that for sure. I might've been about to tell you I wasn't –"

Her breath caught in her throat as his lips began a slow journey along the line of her jaw. Brushing softly over her mouth, any defense she'd been trying so hard to keep intact, crumbled at the huskiness of his voice. "Come on, Jess... kiss me. Put me out of my misery."

And after giving a long sigh of surrender, she did exactly what he asked.

But this kiss was different. *So different.*

He could feel it.

She could feel it.

With this kiss she finally let go, giving into what he had to offer. Her arms wrapping around his neck, she completely relaxed against him. And she held nothing back.

For them, it was a turning point. An unspoken commitment... a crossing of the line into a whole new stage of their relationship.

And it felt *sooooo good...*

Lost in the feeling of holding her in his arms and the promise she had given so freely in her kiss, he didn't want to let her go. Finally lifting his head, but keeping his hold on her, he leaned back against the counter.

He could feel her heartbeat. An echo of his, he'd swear they were beating in perfect harmony. Closing his eyes, he waited as everything inside of him slowly came back down to earth.

He pressed another kiss to her mouth, his voice even more husky. "I should go. If I don't, I'm afraid I won't want to leave at all. I have an early session with the hitting coach tomorrow. Since it will be the first time we meet, being a no show wouldn't be a good option."

His hands sliding into her hair to bring her closer, he searched her face. "And now... about that favor I wanted to ask you. Tomorrow night. Are you free?"

"I think so?"

During the day she had promised Crystal she'd help out at the shop. But as far as tomorrow night? She was pretty sure she didn't have any plans. But after the kiss they shared, still wreaking complete havoc with her mind, she was finding it hard to think.

He smiled at her dazed expression, her face scrunched up in thought. This had him wanting to kiss her all over again.

Tucking her hair behind her ear, he nodded. "I'm going to take that as a yes. I'd like you to be my date for a wedding. It's one of the guys on the team. He invited me yesterday and I wasn't sure if this was something I wanted to do. But now? I'm thinking, with you, it could be fun. From what I heard, the bride has turned the whole event into a wedding-slash-Christmas extravaganza. Formal attire required, the works. Luckily, I have a tux."

He grinned. "My mom insisted I get one when—"

He paused mid-sentence. He wasn't going to tell her this was when he won the American League MVP award. He didn't want to sound like he was bragging. He hadn't even kept the award. He gave it to his parents, telling them they deserved it more than he did.

He cleared his throat. "Well, let's just say, my mom believes every man should have a tuxedo hanging in their closet. Just in case."

As you can imagine, this news was enough to send Jessie in a panic, her mind grabbing right on to his comment about formal attire. This had her scrambling to remember if she'd brought anything with her she could wear.

You're pretty sure you didn't.

Only a few weeks ago, Poppy had borrowed the one formal dress she did have. But since she couldn't remember packing it up with all the rest of her things, this meant it was probably still hanging in Poppy's closet.

Along with all of the other items she had borrowed and somehow forgot to return.

"Jess?" His finger slipping under her chin, he tipped her face up to his. "So, what do you think? Will you go with me?"

She frowned. "I guess I could..."

He chuckled. "*Hmm...* this wasn't exactly the kind of response I'd hoped for. But I'll take it. Even though a little more enthusiasm might have been nice."

He reached for her hand and taking her with him, he headed for the front door. After he slipped into his coat, he framed her face with his hands, pressing a soft kiss to her forehead.

"And now, I really do need to leave. I'll pick you up around five-thirty. Okay?"

She nodded. "Yes, five-thirty."

She was smiling as she watched him run to his car.

And she was still smiling after she made sure the fire was out and had turned off the lights. Running up stairs, she gave a sigh of relief when she saw Crystal's bedroom light was still on.

She knocked on the door.

In bed and reading a book, Crystal glanced up, a smile on her face. "Did Max leave?"

Making her way across the room and settling on the foot of the bed, Jessie nodded. "Yes, he did."

She smiled. "Whatcha reading?"

"It's a cookbook I ordered. All About Coffee Cakes. Can you believe there really is such a book?" She peered more closely at

Jessie. "What's up? I have a feeling you didn't come in here just to ask me what I'm reading."

Jessie cleared her throat, a shy smile on her face. "Now don't go crazy on me, but do you have a formal dress I can borrow? Max asked if I'd go to a wedding with him tomorrow night. It's one of the guys on the team. Supposedly, the bride requested formal attire and I don't have anything that would work. Nor would I be able to find something in such a short time."

Slapping her book shut, Crystal grinned. "I knew it, I knew it."

Jessie shook her head. "*Crystal...*"

Crystal shrugged. "Okay, so I didn't know he'd ask you to a wedding. But It's so obvious he's crazy about you."

Jessie could feel her cheeks getting hotter by the second. "Oh, I don't think so. He only wants to go to this wedding and have a little fun. We're going as friends."

This isn't entirely true. But you're certainly no going to let Crystal know this.

Crystal was shaking her head. "As smart and confident you are as a lawyer, how is it you're such a dimwit when it comes to love?"

Jessie grabbed one of the pillows from the bed and threw it at her. She was laughing. "Stop it. I'm not a dimwit. It's only that I've learned to be more cautious. I like to have all the facts before I commit to anything. Now, back to my question. Do you have something I can wear, or don't you?"

Crystal pointed at the closet. "On the far-left side, in a grey garment bag, is the dress I bought to wear to the annual awards dinner Joe always gets an invited to in September."

She pointed to her baby bump. "But then this happened. I bought the dress almost a year ago because I fell in love with it the moment I saw it in the store. It's a jumpsuit, but since the fabric is so soft and flowing, you'd never guess. Check it out."

Retrieving the garment bag from the closet, Jessie pulled out the jumpsuit.

The fabric was a cross between an iridescent silver and blue, depending on how it hit the light. The v-neck bodice was fitted to the waist, featuring a woven pattern of the chiffon fabric in the front and dipping low in the back. The skirt overlay was layers of the same fabric. Any move of the dress sent the skirt flowing, the fabric shimmering in the light.

"Oh my gosh, Crystal... this is beautiful. Are you sure you want to lend it to me?"

"Of course. Try it on, so we can make sure it fits." She frowned. "I never got shoes, though."

Out of the dress she'd been wearing and already slipping into the jumpsuit, Jessie grinned. "That's okay, I think I have the perfect shoes."

After checking out her refection in the full-sized mirror on the back of the bedroom door, she glanced over at Crystal. "So, what do you think?"

Crystal grinned. "I believe it will only take one look at you and Max will be speechless." She frowned down at her stomach. "At least someone gets to wear the dress. The rate I'm going here, I seriously wonder if I ever will."

Jessie gave her a big hug. "I'm sure you will."

Crystal responded with a sly look. "Maybe at your wedding?"

"Crystal..."

She shrugged. "I'm just sayin'..."

Still in the pantsuit, Jessie gathered up her clothes and headed for the door. "On that note, I am going to bed. Goodnight."

"Goodnight to you, too."

Jessie turned out the light and crawled into bed.

She had just pulled the quilt up to her chin and closed her eyes when she abruptly sat up and grabbed her phone from the nightstand.

She typed in lavender rose and hit search. Scrolling down, she found a link about the history and meaning of flowers.

She scrolled down the list and there it was... lavender rose. This description followed.

The giving of a lavender rose is a sign of enchantment and love at first sight. Giving someone such a rose is a way to express not only your romantic feelings, but your intentions as well. Since the color purple is also traditionally associated with royalty, different shades of lavender roses may also suggest an air of regal majesty and splendor.

She read it again.

Enchantment?

Love at first sight?

Maybe Max misunderstood what the florist told him?

She checked out a few more links about lavender roses.

They all basically said the same thing.

Setting the phone on the nightstand and burrowing back under the quilt, she stared into the darkness.

Enchantment?

Love at first sight?

It took her a long time to fall asleep.

When she did, her dreams were all about weddings, lavender snow and stolen kisses in the night.

CHAPTER 13

Christmas isn't a season, it's a feeling.
~ Anonymous

A light snow was falling when Max arrived to pick up Jessie for the wedding. Turning off the ignition, he peered out the windshield at the sky. Maybe it was his imagination, but the clouds looked a lot darker and heavier than when he left the hotel.

He was trying not to think about the heavy snow warnings the weather channel had been forecasting all morning and afternoon.

Splat...

A snowball hit the windshield, followed by a loud yell.

Slowly emerging from the car, his hands up in surrender, Max grinned over at Jackson. He was holding another snowball, ready to throw it in his direction.

He laughed. "Hey, buddy... I call a truce. It's not a fair fight when I'm dressed like this."

After throwing the snowball as far as he could, watching as it landed in the neighbors driveway, Jackson grinned. "*Awww...* okay. But just wait until next time. I'll get you then."

Max was shaking his head. "With that awesome throw you just made, it looks like I'll need to up my practice. But why are you out here in the dark?"

"I was waiting for you. And I was shoveling the sidewalk. My mom said she'd pay me so I'd have money to buy Christmas presents."

He glanced over at the sidewalk. "But I don't think it did any good. Look, it's already covered with snow again."

"Hey... every little bit helps." Max put his arm around him. "Come on, let's go inside. Your cheeks look like they're frozen. You need some hot chocolate or something."

Jackson pulled open the front door and stomping the snow off his boots, he let out a yell loud enough to be heard three houses away. "Jessie, Max is here."

Wiping her hands on a dish towel, Crystal came from the kitchen, smiling when she saw Max. "My, my... don't you look handsome." She shook her head, giving a long sigh. "What is it about a man in a tux? That and a uniform... gets me every time."

She waved towards the living room. "Have a seat, Jessie should be right down."

Sinking down on the sofa with a big sigh, she looked over at Max "So, while we're waiting, tell me... who's getting married? Is he a good friend of yours?"

Little did Max know, Jessie had been ready for the last fifteen minutes. Maybe more like twenty-five minutes. And if she had her say, they would already be out the door and on their way to the wedding.

But, no... Crystal insisted she make Max wait a few minutes before she came downstairs. And what was the reasoning behind this? She needed to make an entrance, she was told.

For heaven's sake, it's not like you and Max are going to prom or something. You're only helping him out, filling in as his date for this wedding. Not a big deal.

Leaning in towards the mirror, she checked her lipstick to make sure it hadn't smeared. It hadn't. Then she forced a smile on her face, sort of like a practice social smile for later.

She groaned.

Oh geeez... not your best. Looked like more of a grimace than a smile.

Pacing back and forth because heaven forbid she sit down on the bed and wrinkle the fabric ~ this coming as another warning from Crystal ~ she went over and put her ear to the door.

She could hear Crystal's voice.

But *only* Crystal's voice.

This wasn't good. If she didn't get down there to stop her, Max was going to find out every family secret they had.

After one final look in the mirror, she headed for the stairs. Defying Crystal's orders to make a slow and graceful descent, she ran down the stairs, catching her heel on the last step. Miraculously, she was able to grab onto the banister, turning this into a fancy little leap.

A huge grin on his face, Jackson put his hands to his head. "*Wow...* Aunt Jessie, you look hot."

Crystal shot him a horrified glance. "*Jackson...*"

He scratched his head. "But that's a compliment, isn't it?"

She put her finger to her lips. "*Shh...*"

It didn't really matter what Jackson had said. Or for that matter, what Crystal said.

Because Max hadn't heard a single word. Rising to his feet and his eyes locked with Jessie's, he headed straight to her. Unaware of the silence now in the room, he stopped right in front of her, his gaze slowly traveling over her before he gently reached out to run his fingertips along the neckline of her dress. The tremor racing through her at his touch brought on his faint smile, his comment that followed, a soft murmur. "Beautiful, just beautiful."

He slowly took it all in. Her eyes now an even more stunning shade of blue, beckoned to him. If he could, he'd gaze into them forever. Her hair, curling in soft waves to her shoulders, the blush in her cheeks... all of this together, was perfection.

Framing the side of her face in his hand, the kiss he gave her was gentle, almost as if he was afraid to even touch her.

And this was because, in a way, he was. In his eyes she was beautiful, more so than any woman he had ever known. If anyone were to ask him, he'd tell them she lit up the room, her beauty shining like all of the stars in the sky combined.

That she had agreed to be his date for this wedding, had him feeling like he was the luckiest man in the world.

His whisper brushed across her cheek. "If we were alone, I'd give you a kiss to show how you make me feel. But even then, I don't think it would be enough."

This wasn't like him. No woman had ever been able to bring this kind of reaction from him. He usually found he was searching for compliments, trying to come up with the right words.

This had her blushing even more. She wanted to give in, tell him to forget about Crystal and Jackson. So what if they weren't alone? She was more than ready for his kiss.

That she was even thinking this was alarming. She wasn't one to so openly display her feelings. Her career had made her cautious, careful to always maintain a reserved front. But never had it prepared her how to respond to moment like this.

If you let down your guard, you'll be lost.

It was a risk... *way* too much of a risk.

Sending a frantic glance over towards where her coat was hanging on the coat rack, she tried to slip around him.

Even with the short time they'd spent together, Max had become pretty good at sensing Jessie's sudden changes of mood. And by the look of panic on her face, he knew she was having a hard time dealing with how she was feeling.

He smiled.

Yeah, she wanted you to kiss her.

And this was scaring her to death.

Heck, he wanted to tell her it scared him, too.

But this is good. This means you're not the only one swept up in this sudden whirlwind of feelings.

Gently taking hold of her arm, he smiled down at her. "Let me get your coat. With it snowing like it is, we should get going."

Within minutes, they were out the door, with Crystal's repeated reminders to be careful, ringing in their ears.

Jackson watched until the lights of the car were swallowed up in the now rapidly increasing flurries. He turned to Crystal. "Mom, I feel like we're in one of those snow globes."

She smiled. "It does look like that, doesn't it? I hope it doesn't develop into this storm they're talking about." She shook her head, sending another worried glance out the window. "Come on, I made pizza for dinner. I hope you're hungry."

He followed her into the kitchen and plopping down into one of the chairs, he watched as she took the pizza out of the oven. There was a puzzled expression on his face. "Mom? What was wrong with Aunt Jessie? She looked like she didn't even want to be with Max. Did he do something? Doesn't she like him?"

Crystal put the pizza cutter down and leaning against the sink, she studied him. "Oh, I'm pretty sure she likes him. But she doesn't know what to do about it. Sometimes when people are afraid to show what they're truly feeling, they either get angry or act like they don't care. They call this putting your guard up."

She looked over at Jackson.

He looked completely confused.

She laughed. "I guess I didn't explain it very good, did I?" She sighed. "This is when I really miss your dad. He'd know what to say."

She smiled. "I guess you could say Aunt Jessie and Max look like they have fallen in love."

Jackson's fist shot up into the air. "*Yes*... wait until I tell the guys he's going to be my uncle."

Picking up the pizza cutter, Crystal pointed it at him. "Oh, no, no, no... don't you dare. A man like Max gets a lot of press and if they got hold of news like this?"

She shook her head. "*Oh, lordy*... Aunt Jessie would die."

She sent him a very serious look. "You understand what I'm telling you, right?"

Definitely not happy with this, he reluctantly nodded, "Yeah, I understand."

She smiled. "Good. Now, can you please get the salad out of the fridge? Because I don't know about you, but I'm ready to eat. I'm starving."

After Max backed out of the driveway, he glanced over at Jessie. Her hands clenched in her lap, she was staring straight ahead. This, along with the fact she hadn't said much of anything since they got in the car, spelled trouble. He hadn't grown up with two sisters to not know this.

She looked like she was on her way to a funeral, not a wedding.

He briefly closed his eyes.

Geeez... this wasn't the way you envisioned the evening would start. You've got to do something...

He pulled over to the curb, put the car in park and since it was still snowing, he turned on the hazard lights.

She glanced over at this, to be met with his tentative smile. "What's wrong, Jess?"

She opened her mouth, to then shut it again, shaking her head.

He reached over and catching her chin with his hand, he turned her face to his. "Jess... I feel it, too. And I don't know about you, but I'm finding it a little overwhelming. One minute I want to kiss you and never let go. The next minute I want to just take off and run."

A wry smile twisted his lips. "But I have a feeling I'd be back before you even knew I had left."

For a long moment, they remained caught up in each other's gaze.

She finally drew in a deep breath, her response barely audible. "I think... well, what I think I'd prefer..." She briefly closed her eyes. "What I've decided I want you to do... is kiss me. Not, as you put it... take off and run. I really—"

He swooped in, her words swallowed up in his kiss.

It was a loud and annoying sound of a horn from a disgruntled driver as he maneuvered around them, Max finally lifted his head.

He chuckled. "*Ah*, Jessie... see what I mean? One look in your eyes and I lose all track of everything." He pressed a quick kiss to her cheek before he glanced in the rearview mirror, putting the car in gear. "We need to get out of here before we get someone else all riled up."

He grinned over at her. "It would also be nice to make it to this wedding before the whole thing is over. As long as the weather stays like this, we should be fine. But since it looks like I'll need to concentrate on driving, I want you to talk to me. About anything. Ok? Just talk... listening to the sound of your voice will make the drive a breeze."

CHAPTER 14

"*S*o, what do you think?"

His arm draped over the back of her chair, Max was grinning as he gazed down at Jessie. This was because the expression on her face more than indicated what her opinion was of the lavishly decorated venue.

But he still wanted to hear what she had to say.

She gazed around the room. "I know I shouldn't say this, but it all seems so unnecessary. I thought the ceremony was lavish, but this?" She shook her head again.

The room was like a winter wonderland, but there was so much going on, it was overwhelming. Lights were blinking everywhere... in the multitude of trees scattered about the room and in the netting draped across the ceiling.

Each table featured a towering centerpiece made up of twigs, clear glass balls and more lights. The table tops were mirrored and the white place settings were centered with a small white poinsettia.

Max reached over to link his fingers with his. "So... what you're saying, you aren't into big weddings?"

"Oh, Max... I think most women have dreams of a big wedding. But certainly not to this extent. I can only imagine how much this cost, thinking how the money could have been used for so many other things." Her eyes lit up. "Such as replacing the gifts that were stolen from the community center."

She hesitated, studying him. "Were you able to get any response to that?"

Reaching over to tuck her hair behind her ear, his fingers gently going on to trace the line of her jaw, he smiled. "Yeah, I spread the word, made some calls. Hopefully, by tomorrow we'll get some feedback." He gazed slowly around the room. "And I agree with you about all of this. It's nice to know we're on the same page, huh?"

He had moved closer, his next words a brush across her cheek. "I'm glad you decided to come with me tonight. I hope—"

"Excuse me, Jazzy... or is it Janie?"

They both looked over to see this was coming from Margo. One of the women seated at their table, she was motioning to Jessie.

When they had first been seated for dinner, she immediately began firing questions at Jessie ~ how did she meet Max, where did she live, what did she do for a living and so on. It was only after Jessie told her she was a lawyer, the questions finally stopped. Instead, she kept a close eye on Jessie throughout the meal, a calculating expression on her face.

Now trying to hide her annoyance, Jessie gave her a bright smile, her eyebrows raised. "It's Jessie, remember?" She didn't want to be mean, but come on... she had told her this at least three times, maybe four.

Margo gave her a dismissive wave. "Whatever, Jessie, Janie... does it really matter? Come with me to the women's lounge. The dancing is going to start soon and I think we could both use a little bit of a freshening up, don't you?"

She had come around the table and was now standing next to Jessie, waiting.

Not wanting to make a scene, Jessie stood.

Max immediately jumped to his feet, a worried look on his face. "Jess, you don't have to go."

She smiled at him. "It's okay, I won't be long. Save me a dance, ok?"

He leaned in to press a kiss to her cheek, his answer a whisper in her ear. "They're all yours, since the only woman I want to dance with is you. I'll be waiting."

He watched them walk away, before slowly sinking back down into his seat.

"I don't know what George sees in her. She's a troublemaker, that one." Max turned to see this had come from Adam. Seated next to him, he was also one of the guys on the team.

Glancing over to where the two women had disappeared, Max chuckled, shaking his head. "I'm not worried. Jessie can handle her."

He nodded. "Yep, I'll bet on her any day."

After almost knocking over an elderly woman when she shoved open the door to the women's lounge, Margo headed straight for the large mirrored vanity.

This left Jessie with the task of apologizing to the shaken woman, making sure she wasn't hurt.

Besides them, the lounge was empty, something Jessie found a little concerning. She had a feeling Margo had brought her here for a reason. And it had nothing to do with freshening up their make-up.

She watched as Margo began pulling items from the hidden pockets in the skirt of her gown.

Mascara, eye shadow, cover stick, blush, lipstick... you name it, she had it on her.

She made eye contact with Jessie in the mirror. "Do you like my pockets? This was what sold me on this dress. I can fit every-thing I need in them and more." Dabbing something under her eyes, she watched herself in the mirror as she spoke. "So, you're the woman everyone is gossiping about around the league. The mysterious wife of Max Kirby."

Jessie's mouth dropped open before she abruptly closed it. In an attempt to be a vague as possible, she sent Margo a brief smile. "Really? *Wow*... so this is the news, huh?" She shook her head. "Max told me how quickly things get around, but I guess I didn't quite believe him." She shrugged. "Oh well, neither of us have anything to hide."

Slapping blush on her face, something Jessie wanted to tell her was going to put her in a whole new category of made up if she wasn't careful, Margo sent her a calculating look. "You do know he was practically engaged only a short time ago, don't you?"

She nodded before she picked up her mascara. "Yep, to Mandy Winters. But she broke it off and got engaged to one of the other guys on the team shortly after."

She uncapped her mascara, leaning in closer to the mirror. "But she's realized she made a mistake. So, she called off the engagement and has plans to meet with Max in a few days." She sent Jessie a sly look. "She is staying with me. We've been friends for years."

She shook her head before she moved to the other eye "I have never seen a man as heartbroken as Max was when Mandy told him it was over. He was so devastated, he disappeared for days."

She stilled, the mascara wand in mid-air as she stared at her reflection in the mirror. Then, giving a shiver, she glanced over at Jessie. "True love... this is exactly what they had... something you don't see all that often these days."

Almost angrily slamming the mascara down on the counter, she picked up her lipstick and applied a heavy layer. After blowing a kiss to her refection, she stuffed everything back in her pockets.

Jessie had nothing to say. She knew she shouldn't take what Margo just told her as the truth, but again, it very well could be.

What she did know? She'd definitely feel so much better if it had been Max who had ended the relationship.

When she realized Margo was watching her, no doubt wondering why she had nothing to say, she studied her. After she did this just long enough to make her feel uncomfortable, she spoke. "And why have you decided to tell me this?"

Her concentration now on her hair, Margo sighed. "If you saw Mandy and Max together, you'd agree with everyone else they're the perfect couple. She's beautiful. In fact, she was Miss California a few years ago. It also doesn't hurt that her brother is also a baseball player and her father is a co-owner of the Minnesota team."

She frowned, shaking her head. "He wasn't happy when Max left for Cleveland. I know for a fact, he'd do anything to get Max back on the team."

At this point Jessie decided it would be best if she left. She glanced over at the small clock on vanity. Her hand going to her mouth, she gave a little gasp. "Oh my, look at the time. I promised Max I would make this short." She shrugged, giving Margo what she hoped was a dreamy smile. After all, this hadn't been one of the smiles she'd practiced earlier in the mirror. "He hates when I'm away from him too long."

She headed for the door, sending Margo a glance over her shoulder, "Are you coming?"

Confronted with Margo's furious expression, she quickly opened the door. "Okay, then... I can see you're not. Take your time. I'll see you back at the table."

Slipping out of the room, she began walking as fast as her heels would allow.

She frowned. Was she a little worried?

Yes... yes, you are. Very worried.

How could she not be? This whole situation with Max was beginning to feel so unreal. Almost as though she had been caught up in a dream, or acting a part in some kind of sitcom. Nothing seemed real.

So, you need to keep things in perspective.

It was time to go back to her original plan... starting with getting Crystal through the holidays. Then she would work at straightening out her own life. How and where this would take place, she wasn't quite sure.

But, what she did know? She wasn't quite ready to give up the life she had worked so hard for... at least not just for a man.

Hmm... if you say so.

But right now, as long as she was here, she wanted to dance with Max. She had a feeling he would be the perfect dance partner.

And even though this wedding was over the top, it was what any woman would imagine as the perfect setting for any fairy tale.

Was this her enchanted evening moment? The one every girl should be allowed to have at least once in her lifetime?

If it was, she wanted that dance even more.

Max checked his watch.

Jessie had been gone for fifteen minutes.

Not that he was worried about her. His problem right now was with this Margo. He didn't have a very good feeling about her. He'd be blind not to have noticed the glaring looks she kept sending Jessie during dinner. He also couldn't shake the feeling he'd met her at one time. But for the life of him, he couldn't remember when or where.

But this is understandable. She's the type of woman you'd want to forget.

A hand coming down on his shoulder, he glanced up to see it was Adam. "Hey, buddy. We're leaving. I just heard they closed the freeway because the weather has taken a turn for the worse and we have almost an hour drive as it is. Then I have to drive the babysitter home. So, enjoy the rest of the night."

He nodded towards where the bride and groom were in the

midst of a heated argument. "Looks like things are getting a little heated. We all tried to tell him to hold off on the wedding, make sure this is what he wanted, but you know how that goes…" He was shaking his head as he began walking away. "I'll see you around. Drive carefully when you leave."

As if to prove his point, the bride suddenly burst into tears and went running from the room.

At the same time, Max saw Jessie coming towards him. Their eyes meeting, he smiled, an everything-was-right-in-the-world feeling coursing through him when she smiled back.

This was when he knew… she would always be the only woman he'd want to be waiting for. As long as he had her with him, it didn't matter what crazy plans this life had in store for them.

And how can you be sure about this?

He reached for her hand and the shiver, or maybe it was more of a spark, that raced through them, gave him his answer.

Yep, you're sure.

This sudden revelation leaving him feeling a little rattled, he had to clear his throat. "Hey, is everything okay? What happened to Margo?"

She scrunched up her face. "I think she's still working on her make-up." She glanced back at the door. "I almost got run over by the bride. She appeared to be very upset about something. Did something happen while I was gone?"

For a long moment, he didn't answer. This was because he was beginning to wonder why they were even here, when he'd much rather spend time with her alone.

He slowly shook his head. "From what little I've been told, this isn't exactly a marriage made in heaven, but more about the event itself. Pretty sad, I'd have to say. He seems like a nice guy, but maybe not too bright?"

He ran his hand through his hair, his glance going over to the entrance of the room. "I also heard the weather has gotten much worse."

"It is. When I was out in the lobby, I saw some people were leaving."

He slowly gazed around the room before he turned back to her. "Would you mind if we left, too? Between the weather, the fighting and everything else they have going on here, I think I've had enough."

She hesitated, sending a quick glance over to where the band was tuning up.

I guess this means you're not going to get that dance you wanted. No fairy tale ending tonight, it seems.

As if he read her mind, a slow smile curved his lips. "I promise I'll make it up to you. Dinner, dancing, whatever your heart desires."

Okay, then.

She smiled. "It's a deal."

CHAPTER 15

They told me that to make her fall in love,
I had to make her laugh. But every time she laughs,
I'm the one who falls in love...
~ Anonymous

*M*ax pulled out of the parking garage right into a solid world of white. The blowing and swirling snow was relentless, coming right at them.

After barely skidding to a stop at the first light, he smiled over at Jessie. "Something tells me this is going to be a very interesting trip home. I'm going to need you to talk to me again, Jess... just like you did on our drive here, okay?"

So, she started talking.

They had now been driving for almost an hour and Jessie was running out of things to talk about. Up until now, she had filled Max in on almost all the details of her life, probably a lot more than he wanted to know.

And no doubt, a lot of what you should've kept to yourself.

She had rambled on about her childhood. To continue right

on through high school and college, before finishing up with her graduation from law school and moving to Chicago.

Well, he asked you to talk, so, this is what you did.

The condition of the roads had grown worse, the blowing snow making visibility almost non-existent. And now, watching the wipers scrape across the icy windshield, she gave a long sigh, relieved they didn't have much further to go.

Max reached over to trail his fingertips down her cheek. "Again, I'm sorry we had to leave." He sent her a smile. "I guess you'll have to wait a little bit longer to meet everyone."

She huddled deeper in her coat, a smile spreading across her face at what he said.

He wants you to meet everyone?

This had her off and dreaming.

"Jess, honey... keep talking. It shouldn't be much longer."

Resting her head against the back of the seat, she gazed over at him. "*Hmm...* okay. So, have you ever been to Chicago?"

As Max slowly guided the car around the corner and onto the street Crystal's house was located, he gave a long, relieved sigh.

He glanced over at Jessie. "I don't know about you, but I can't wait to get out of this car. Only a few minutes and we'll be home."

Unfortunately, the flashing red and blue lights in his rearview mirror were an indication it wasn't going to be this easy.

Max slowed to a stop. He then watched as Captain Bobby Gunn emerged from the police cruiser.

Dropping his head down on the steering wheel, he groaned. "You've got to be kidding me. It's looks like it's none other than your friend, Captain Gunn, one of Blossom Fall's finest, is on the job tonight. I Wonder why he's stopping me? It can't be for speeding."

Lifting his head, he gazed over at Jessie. "So close... we were so, so close..."

Jessie's eyes were huge, pleading with him. "Oh, no… I'm so sorry. Please be careful what you say to him. Remember, he takes his job very seriously."

"Yeah, yeah, yeah… how could I forget? Mr. Law and Order." This came in a mumble as Max opened the window.

Bobby leaned down to peer into the car. After shining his flashlight right in Max's face, he aimed it at Jessie. Finally turning off the flashlight, he loudly cleared his throat. "Not a good night to get all dressed up for a drive around town, is it? With your Minnesota plates, and knowing how the weather can be in that fine state, I'd think you'd be more selective about your choice of activity on a night like tonight. I'd also think their laws would be the same as they are here… a stop sign meaning stop, not slow down."

Checking his irritation, Max's answer came out surprisingly casual. "You're right on all accounts. I might not have come to a complete stop just a moment ago, but under the circumstances, I felt it was better to keep moving. There were no other vehicles around and I didn't want to take the chance of getting stuck. This has been a traumatic experience for Jessie and my only goal is to get her home."

Concern crossing his face, Bobby peered over at Jessie again. "And you're all right, ma'am?"

Jessie gave him a big smile. "Bobby, it's me, Jessie." When he frowned at her familiarity, she sighed. "Sorry, Captain Gunn. Believe me, I'm fine. We went to a wedding and had no idea the weather would get this bad. So, now we only want to get home." She nodded towards where they'd normally be able to see Crystal's house if it weren't for the blowing snow.

Bobby straightened, sending Max a curt nod. "I'll let you off this time. But try to be more careful in the future."

He jerked his head over at Jessie. "We treasure each and every one of our residents here in Blossom Falls, our primary aim to keep everyone safe." He tipped his hat. "Enjoy the rest of your evening."

Watching in his rearview mirror, Max waited until he was back inside the police cruiser before he pulled away from the curb. He chuckled, while at the same time he was shaking his head. "Man, I guess everyone should be as dedicated to their job as he is."

The words were no sooner out of his mouth when the red and blue flashing lights began following right behind them. He groaned. "You've got to be kidding me... is this really necessary? I'm surprised he hasn't hit the siren."

As if on cue, there was a short wail of the siren, almost like a farewell gesture as Max pulled into the driveway.

They looked over at each other.

She shrugged. "What can I say? Except... Welcome to Blossom Falls."

They both burst out laughing.

As he opened the car door, Max was shaking his head.

As crazy as it may seem, he was looking forward to what might happen next.

CHAPTER 16

*S*nuggled together under a quilt on the sofa, a big bowl
of popcorn between them, Crystal and Jackson were
watching the movie Elf.

The sudden flash of lights and short burst of a siren sent
Jackson diving off the sofa and over to the window.

His voice high with excitement, he glanced over his shoulder
at Crystal. "Mom... it's Max and Jessie. And there's a police car
following them."

Believe it or not, Crystal scrambled off the sofa almost as fast
as Jackson. Joining him at the window, her hand went to her
mouth. "*Oh, no... I wonder what happened?*"

They watched as Max got out of the car and ran around to
open the passenger door. This was followed by what sounded
like a heated discussion between them when Jessie started to get
out of the car.

Max scooped her up in his arms and after cutting off any of
her further protests with a long kiss, he began trudging through
the snow to the front door.

Jackson glanced up at Crystal. "*Awww, man...* did he have to
kiss her? Really? See, this is what always happens. Girls are bad
news."

Laughing as she went over to open the door, she turned to point her finger at him. "Now don't you dare say anything. I happen to think it's wonderful. They're perfect together."

She put her finger to her lips. "Remember... not a word."

"Max, put me down." These words no sooner came flying out of Jessie's mouth when the door flew open, Crystal's anxious glance traveling over both of them.

"What happened?"

Gently dropping Jessie to the floor and closing the door, Max shrugged. "As you can see, the weather prompted our decision to leave the reception early. And now, it seems my attempt to be nice is not at all appreciated by Jess, here."

Struggling out of her coat, Jessie gave a huffy sigh. "I am perfectly capable of walking."

Quickly moving to help her, ignoring her attempts to avoid him, Max shook his head. "Not in the snow and with the shoes you're wearing."

He rolled his eyes at Crystal. "Has she always been so stubborn? Or is it just me?"

Crystal grinned. "No, it's not you. And, yes, she's always been this way."

She glanced out the window, where Bobby's patrol car was now slowly driving away, the lights still flashing. "Why was Bobby following you?"

After Jessie explained what happened, Crystal let out a big sigh of relief. "Well, the important thing is you're home. You made the right choice by leaving. They are predicting blizzard like conditions all night and most of tomorrow."

She smiled at them. "Did you have dinner?" At Max's nod, she smiled. "But I bet you didn't have dessert, did you. I brought home one of my cinnamon pecan coffee cakes. It's really good with ice cream..."

He laughed. "Now, you know there's no way I'm going to

pass up an offer like that. But only if you all have some. Jackson, too."

Jackson grinned. "I'm in."

Crystal watched as Max shrugged off his jacket and loosened his tie before she motioned to Jackson. "I want you to start getting everything ready while I go upstairs and get Max something more comfortable to wear."

Her gaze traveled over him. "It looks like you and Joe are about the same size."

She raised an eyebrow. "Unless you'd rather stay in your tux?"

Jackson grinned. "You better do as she says. Trust me, once she makes up her mind about something, it's a done deal. I should know."

Max sent him a wink. "I have no intention of refusing. I'll be more than happy to get out of this tux."

Crystal started up the stairs. "Good. Jess, come with me and you can change, too."

Once they were upstairs, her hands on her hips, Jessie glared at Crystal. "What are you doing? Inviting him to stay the night?"

Crystal gave her a long stare, enough to make her feel guilty. She sighed. "Come on, Criss... It's so obvious you're trying to throw us together and it's embarrassing. The last thing either of us are thinking about is falling in love with each other."

Crystal snorted. "This coming from the woman who just shared a passionate kiss with a man as he carried her through a raging blizzard so she wouldn't get her feet wet." She gave Jessie another one of her annoying know-it-all looks. "And if that isn't love, I don't know what it could be."

Jessie groaned... "First of all, it wasn't a 'raging' blizzard. Second of all, what was I supposed to do? If I tried to stop him, he might have dropped me. He was just trying to be nice."

"*Hmm*... nice. That kiss he gave you looked like it was more than just nice." Crystal shrugged. "But, okay… whatever you say. I'll try not to interfere in the future."

Jessie sighed. "I find this hard to believe. You've been at it all my life, so why would you stop now?"

Crystal sighed. "*Oh, Jess…* I just don't want you to pass up on what could be something so wonderful. I see the way Max looks at you. And even if you think you're not ready, from what I can see, he's already decided you're the one. And, come on… what woman wouldn't die for a man like him?"

Watching Crystal rummage through the dresser drawer, trying to find something for Max to wear, Jessie frowned. "And this is the problem. I don't want to compete against all of these women, to only lose him in the end. I don't think I could handle it…"

She sank down on the bed, her voice fading off into silence.

Crystal turned around, her eyes wide. "Oh Jessie, you've already fallen for him, haven't you? And now you're doing what you've done all your life. Instead of enjoying the moment, you're already worrying about what's coming next. Go for it, Jess. Live in the moment. I have a feeling you and Max are meant to be."

A smile suddenly tweaked the corner of her mouth. "I take it this means Bobby is now out of the running. You should know he's been hinting lately about running for mayor. This means whoever marries him could eventually refer to herself as the first lady of Blossom Falls." She laughed. "Robin is probably the one who put the idea in his head. She's had her eye on him ever since she got divorced."

Jessie started to laugh. "Robin is more than welcome to him. She'd be perfect as the mayor's wife. They would do great things together."

A pair of flannel pajama pants and a tee shirt draped over her arm, Crystal headed for the door. "I'm taking these down to Max. Hurry up and get changed, okay?"

She left, only to poke her head back into the room, her words an exaggerated whisper. "I mean it… think about what I said."

Alone in the room, Jessie stared over at the mini lighted Christmas tree Crystal had set up on the dresser.

It was only when she heard Max laughing at something Jackson said, she made a move to get changed.

And, yeah... she was smiling.

Jessie found Max settled on the sofa watching TV. He smiled, patting the space next to him. "Hey, come on over and join me."

Her conversation with Crystal still fresh in her mind, she was now a bundle of nerves. She smiled, slowly inching her way towards the kitchen. "I should probably see if Crystal needs my help."

Almost leaping from the sofa, he was at her side in an instant. Taking her hand, he led her back to the sofa, pulling her down next to him. "Nope, you're staying right here with me. Crystal and Jackson don't need your help. But, I need your company."

He put his arm around her, giving a long sigh of content-ment. "*Hmm...* here in our pajamas, just you and me. This is so much better than being at a crazy-over-the-top-wedding." Pressing a kiss to the top of her head, there was a smile in his voice. "I swear, every minute I spend with you turns into an adventure. Never did I think we'd get pulled over by Blossom Falls finest."

She smiled. "I'm just glad Bobby didn't take advantage of his power."

He chuckled. "I'll admit I was a little nervous when I realized he was the one who pulled us over. I was waiting for him to handcuff me and cart me off to jail. If only so I couldn't be with you."

She laughed. "Oh, I don't think he'd go that far."

"Jessie, come on... the guy has a major crush on you. Prob-ably has for years. He couldn't be more obvious."

She sighed. "He did come to see me right before I left for

college. He told me I could call him if I needed any help. I was angry and told him I didn't need anything from him."

His eyebrows raised, Max shook his head. "You? Angry? Because someone offered their help? *Hmm...* I find that hard to believe."

Before she could respond, and he knew darn well she would, he captured her mouth in a leisurely kiss.

Unfortunately, Jackson picked that very moment to come into the room. He was carrying a tray holding the promised dessert.

He groaned.

Loudly, he did this.

"Oh geeez... not again. I don't understand what you two see in this kissing thing."

After pressing a brief kiss to Jessie's cheek, Max was laughing as he jumped up to take the tray from Jackson. "Whoa, buddy... this is heavy. You must be pretty strong."

He reached over and roughed his hair with his hand. "And the kiss? Trust me, one day you'll understand completely."

Max set his empty plate on the table before he smiled over at Crystal. "You are an amazing baker. Have you ever thought of expanding the business, maybe selling them on-line?"

Crystal sighed. "Joe keeps telling me the same thing." She nodded over towards Jessie. "Jessie, too. But I don't know. I'm afraid they'll lose their hometown appeal. Right now, I have more than enough business to keep me busy. And I wouldn't even know how to get started with an online business, nor do I have the resources. Military salaries don't give you much extra to play around with."

"I'm pretty sure you could get a small business loan. I'd be more than happy to help you with that, put my business degree to good use." He smiled over at Jessie. "And you already have a lawyer to guide you through all the paperwork. I'm sure she'd give you a discount on her fees."

Setting her empty plate next to Max's, Jessie nodded over at Crystal. "You could pay me in cake."

Crystal smiled at both of them before she patted her stomach. "Right now, this baby is all I can handle. Maybe when Joe is finally back home I'll be ready to think about it."

Hauling herself out of her chair, she beckoned to Jackson. "You should've been in bed over an hour ago. Come upstairs with me so I can give you a blanket and pillow to bring to Max."

Her hands on her hips, the warning look she sent Max was one not to be argued with. "You're not going out in this snowstorm. Promise me you won't."

He nodded. "Promise. And thanks…"

She smiled. "Sure, goodnight."

Max found Jessie in the kitchen.

She was loading the dishwasher.

Déjà vu…

Yeah, you could get used to this.

He was smiling as he moved behind her, wrapping his arms around her. When she slowly relaxed against him, he pulled her closer, pressing a kiss in the curve of her neck.

When another one of those shivers skittered through them, he smiled. There was a huskiness in his voice, his breath brushing her ear. "Did you feel that? We've got some serious chemistry going on between us, Jess."

Closing her eyes, she let herself be carried away by the sound of his voice, his words.

"Jess?"

She turned and wrapping her arms around his neck, she searched his face. "You're driving me crazy… and I have a feeling you know this, don't you?" She sighed. "You have me so I can't even think straight and this isn't like—"

He pulled her closer, pressing a kiss to her mouth. "*Shh…* that's the problem, you're thinking too much. Now me? I haven't had a clear thought in my head since I first looked into your eyes. But I don't care."

He shrugged. "It feels good... it feels right. And I plan to enjoy every—"

Her kiss put a stop to whatever he had to say.

His arm along the back of the sofa, his fingers resting on her shoulder, Max pressed a kiss in Jessie's hair. "Did you find anything worth watching?"

Jessie smiled up at him. "*Hmm...* it depends, do you want romance or comedy?"

He hesitated. He definitely needed to be careful of how he answered this. "*Uh...* maybe a little of both?"

She laughed at the uneasy expression on his face before she reached up to kiss his cheek. "Christmas movies. I was thinking more along the line of a Christmas movie."

She picked up the remote and began searching the guide on the TV screen. "But if you want a little of both, I'm sure we can find something."

He was smiling. "A Christmas movie it is, sweetheart. I believe we've already experienced our share of both romance and comedy tonight. And, as promised, I want to make it up to you. Bring on more of the romance... such as dinner, the works. Wherever you'd like to go. Maybe Tuesday?"

She nodded. "I would love that. But you pick the place... I trust you."

Brushing her hair back from her face, his expression turned serious. "*Ah...* you trust me. How much?"

Her smile, even as faint as it was, had him smiling, too. "Jess?"

She gazed up at him. "A lot. I trust you completely. I really do."

And he could see in her beautiful eyes, the different shades of blue so mesmerizing, she meant this.

He cupped her chin in his hand to give her a soft kiss. "Good, I promise not to disappoint. Tuesday it is."

Max glanced down at Jessie. Curled up next to him on the sofa and her head on his shoulder, they were watching a Christmas movie they found on TV.

But it appeared he was now the only one watching the movie.

Jessie was sound asleep.

Grabbing the remote and turning off the TV, he pulled the quilt more securely around them. He knew he should wake her so she could go to bed, but it felt so good having her with him.

It felt more than good.

It felt right.

He closed his eyes. Just ten more minutes... then he'd wake her.

But as we all know, even the most sincere plans can so easily go awry.

CHAPTER 17

The best feeling in the world is when
the person you like, likes you back
~ Anonymous

*J*ackson's laugh is what woke Max. Along with the muted sound of morning cartoons on TV.

Slowly opening his eyes, only to close them against the bright morning light, he yawned, about to give a long stretch.

But this turned out to be impossible. It turned out he was securely wedged between the arm of the sofa and Jessie. Sound asleep and practically on top of him, her head was resting on his chest, her arm flung across his stomach.

Lifting his head, he glanced over to see they were occupying, at the most, only about half of the sofa

Yep, you can't get any closer than this.

It looked like his plan to wake her up so she could go upstairs to bed had never materialized.

A slow grin began to spread across his face.

Smoothing the hair back from her face, his voice was gruff with sleep. "Hey Jess... wake up, baby."

Her lashes barely fluttering, only to close again, he watched as a faint smile flickered across her lips.

He pressed a kiss in her forehead. "Jess, honey... come on, you've got me so wedged up against the arm of this sofa, I can't move. I'm starting to lose feeling in my legs."

This time her lashes flew open and stayed open, her eyes going wide. Struggling into a sitting position she ran her hand through her hair before she sent a wild glance around the room.

Her gaze finally settling on his face, for a few moments she stared at him as though she had no clue of who he was.

He chuckled. "Well, I can see you're not a morning person, are you?" He brushed his knuckles across her cheek. "It looks like we spent the night here. But I slept great. How about you?"

This galvanized her into action, pushing at the blanket in an effort to get off the sofa. "I'm so sorry, so, so, sorry."

Then suddenly angry, she came to an abrupt halt. She began mumbling. "Why didn't you wake me up before you went to sleep? You should have. Or at least tried."

But now her feet had become tangled in the blanket, her attempt to pull them free almost sending her head first to the floor. Pulling her back against him, Matt smiled. "*Hey, hey...* take it easy. Nothing happened. I guess I was just too comfortable to stay awake. In fact, it looks like we both were."

He pressed a kiss to the top of her head. "And I only wanted you to move a little, not leave. You're definitely in no shape to go anywhere until you're a little more awake."

Pouring more cereal into the bowl in front of him, Jackson was watching all of this with interest. He nodded. "Yeah, she needs coffee before you can even think of having a conversation with her. At least this is what mom says."

Jessie stuck her tongue out at him. "Maybe the problem isn't me, you talk too much and I can't get a word in. But speaking of your mom, where is she? Upstairs?"

He shook his head. "No, she went to the shop."

Both Max and Jessie reacted the same, throwing questions at him, one after another.

"What?"

"She went out in this weather?"

"But it's Sunday. The shop is closed."

"How did she get there?"

Jackson stuffed a big spoonful of cereal in his mouth before he answered. "*Geeesh...* cool it. Marilyn's husband came and picked her up." He glanced over at Jessie. "She told me to tell both of you she doesn't need help today, there wasn't much to do. She said you'd only be in the way."

After another spoonful of cereal, he jerked his head over at Max. "And, yeah... your phone has been ringing. I bet it rang about ten times. Mom hooked it up to the charger on the kitchen counter before she left."

"Thanks, Jackson. I better check it out." He stood and reaching for Jessie's hand, he pulled her up off the sofa. He smiled. "And while I'm there, I'm going to make you breakfast."

He grinned. "Breakfast is one thing I can do. I think you'll be pleasantly surprised."

He pressed a kiss to her cheek. His lips going on to trail over her jaw had her moving even closer.

He was having a hard time. With her hair all mussed and her cheeks flushed with sleep, he was pretty sure she had no idea how desirable she looked. To the point he'd give just about anything to tumble her back on the sofa and hold her in his arms for a little while longer.

But you'd want more... you know you would...

So, instead? He gave her a teasing smile. "Unless you need more time to wake up? If so, I'd be more than willing to cuddle with you on the sofa for a little longer, maybe watch some cartoons, or we could just enjoy each other's company..."

His gaze slowly traveled over her face, to finally settle on her mouth. He smiled. "Whatever your heart desires. Jess."

Her heart now beating like crazy, there was no doubt it

desired exactly what he was offering, if not more. Flustered, she shook her head. "No, no... I'm awake now. But, you really want to make me breakfast? How can I refuse an offer like that?"

After he pressed a kiss to her cheek, he waved over at Jackson to get his attention. "Hey, I'm going to need your help, tell me where things are. This will only take a few minutes. Then you can come back and watch the rest of your shows."

Jackson showed Max where to find everything he would need to make breakfast. With the promise there would be enough for him, too, he had gone back to his cartoons.

After Max made sure Jessie had a cup of coffee on the table in front of her, he sent her a big smile. "Okay, so are you ready to watch a pro at work?"

Her chin resting in her hand, she nodded. She was finding it hard to believe she was sitting in her sister's kitchen while watching this incredibly handsome man make breakfast.

And that he was doing this just for her?

This was even more amazing.

He popped the toast in the toaster and after adding the eggs to the skillet, this accomplished with a great deal of fanfare, he turned to give her a big grin. "Impressed?"

She nodded. "Very. There's something so very sexy about a man at work in the kitchen."

He leaned back against the counter, his arms crossed and a spatula in one hand. After he studied her for a few moments, he gave her a slow smile. It was a smile that sent a shiver through her, making her heart give a little leap. Almost as if to get his attention... let him know she was his.

No questions asked.

A playful look on his face, he set the spatula on the counter. "I'm going to leave this here, since we're both well aware of your tendency to use kitchen items as weapons."

She tilted her head. "*Ah...* but that was when I really didn't know you all that well."

He took a step closer, a smile touching his lips. " Yes, back in my fugitive days, I believe? But... Sexy, huh? So, what you're saying, I only have to feed you and you'll be all mine?"

She nodded, unaware she'd swayed towards him, her lips parted in anticipation.

He, of course, saw this as a definite invitation she wanted him to kiss her. Placing his hands down on the table, he leaned in until their mouths were only a breath away. A soft sigh escaping her, she closed her eyes when his lips brushed over hers in a whisper. "Kiss me, Jess."

"Hey, what's burning?" Jackson's yell had Max abruptly lifting his head to see smoke rising from the toaster. Reaching the counter in record time, he fished the charred pieces of bread out of the toaster and threw them in the trash.

After he put more bread in the toaster, he sent Jessie a teasing grin. "I could blame this on you, but I won't. Not this time."

He turned back to the stove to check on the eggs before he sent her a smile over his shoulder. "For now, since I promised you breakfast, let me finish without any more mishaps. But you can bet I'll collect on that kiss when we're done."

Jessie watched as Max ended the call he was on.

He was smiling.

"Good news?"

He nodded. "Very good news." He glanced over at the clock on the microwave. "A truck is going to be arriving at the community center in about an hour. Loaded with gifts to replace most of those that were taken. They'll need to be wrapped, but all of that—paper, bows and stuff—is also going to be on the truck."

She reached over to give him a big kiss. "Oh my gosh... this is wonderful. You're wonderful."

He grinned.

Her kiss, along with the big smile on her face had him wishing he could have delivered dozens of trucks. "I'd hoped they'd be able to help out, but didn't think they'd come through so big and so fast. Not at this late date."

He pulled her up out of her chair, wrapping his arms around her. Gazing down at her, he smiled. "So, it looks like we have our work cut out for us. You need to call Crystal so she can spread the word. They're going to need a ton of volunteers to help wrap all the gifts."

His head dipping down, he pressed a soft kiss to her face, followed by another one... and then another before he finally ended at her mouth. There was a smile in his voice. "But first, I want to collect on that kiss you owe me."

CHAPTER 18

$\mathcal{M}$ax pulled his car up behind the large truck parked in front of the community center.

He and Jessie watched as a man inside the truck, wearing a Santa hat, kept throwing boxes down to another man, wearing a cowboy hat. After making a dive for the boxes, he began piling them onto a cart.

Both men were laughing when they glanced over to see Max's car. The man in the truck peered over at them, a big grin lighting up his face when he recognized Max.

"Hey, Max... or should I say *ho, ho, ho*... Merry Christmas?"

Max grinned over at Jessie. "That's Kevin Kardell. He's on the team. And the guy with the cowboy hat? That's Sean Young, also on the team. Come on, I want to introduce you to them."

When they reached Sean, Kevin jumped down from the back of the truck to join them.

Max put his arm around Jessie. "Sean, Kevin, I want you to meet Jessie Carter. And be careful what you say. She's a lawyer. So, not only is she beautiful, she's smart, too. No doubt more than the two of you put together."

Kevin scratched his head. "And she chose you?" He glanced over at Sean, an eyebrow raised. "Doesn't make sense, does it?"

Having removed his hat when he greeted Jessie, Sean settled it back on his head, adjusting it just so.

Then he frowned. "Nope, but then again, we're just getting to know the guy. She must see something in him we don't."

He smiled over at Jessie. "You make sure he treats you right. And if he doesn't, feel free to come to one of us and we'll straighten him out."

Jessie laughed. "Thank you, I'll remember this."

She sent a smile up at Max. "So far, I have no complaints."

She gestured towards the truck. "Thank you for this. It would have been awful if we couldn't hand out gifts this year. For some of the kids, this is the highlight of their year."

They all watched as the door of the community center suddenly flew open with a loud bang and Bobby came lumbering down the steps.

Max groaned. "*Oh no,* it's non-other than our fearless leader, Captain Gunn."

Bobby headed straight for Jessie. "Hey, Jessie. Your sister is already here. Jackson, too."

His gaze traveling over to Max, he stared at him for a few moments before he spoke. "I see your buddies are almost done unloading the truck. Since they're doing Blossom Falls a favor, I'll let it pass they parked in a fire lane."

He loudly cleared his throat, satisfied his point had been made. "But the real reason I'm here is because Crystal sent me. She wants me to remind all of you to come and get something to eat before you leave."

He frowned down at Jessie. "Your sister has been waiting for you. You should've called her, Jessie."

Noting the flash of anger in Jessie's eyes at what Bobby said, Max quickly spoke up. "You can blame me for that. I promised to make her breakfast and it took me a lot longer than I anticipated,"

And just like that, all eyes were on Jessie. A blush beginning to fill her cheeks, she started to back away. "I guess I should see what Crystal has lined up for me." She sent Kevin and Sean a bright smile. "It was nice meeting you."

"Yeah, I'm sure we'll be seeing you around." This came from Kevin, along with a big grin.

Sean tipped his hat. "Same here. And remember what we said... we're here if you need us." He followed this with a wink.

She sent them a little wave before she glanced over at Max. "I'll see you inside?"

"Yeah, I'll be there in a few minutes."

She headed for the entrance, with Bobby following right behind her. "Hey, Jessie... wait up."

Kevin waited until they were inside the community center before he glanced over at Max. His grin was a hint of what was to come. "Why do I get the feeling you're up against some serious competition? But I gotta hand it to you with your breakfast comment. That's a definite hands-off claim you gave him."

Sean nodded. "Yep, you, my man, are up against a man of the law. One who is very serious not only about his job, but his women, too. You better watch your step."

Max was shaking his head. "Yeah, tell me about it." He proceeded to tell them about their encounter with Bobby on the way home from the wedding. He chuckled. "I had visions of him carting me off to jail for some made up charges. Between that and the fiasco that was the wedding, it was quite a night."

Sean grinned over at Kevin. "But in the end, he was still able to hold on to the girl. It looks like he is going to fit in just fine."

He nodded over at the entrance to the community center. "You better get in there and stake your claim. We can handle the rest."

"Thanks... I'll see you guys inside."

He had no sooner left when Kevin hoisted himself back in the truck and threw a box to Sean. Just barely managing to catch it before it hit him in the head, Sean sent him a dirty look.

Kevin shrugged. "Come on, you need to pay attention. Let's

see how fast we can finish this up. I don't know about you, but I'm getting hungry."

Sean grinned. "I'm always hungry. Let's do this."

Max found Jessie with Crystal, filling out the gift tags. Coming up behind her, he pressed a kiss right below her ear before he smiled over at Crystal. "Hey, what would you like me to do?"

She pointed over to where Jackson had crawled under the desk in the corner of the room, only his feet visible. She shook her head. "I sent him to bring over the box of ribbons and he dropped it, rolls of ribbon flying everywhere. One of the rolls must have gone under the desk and now he's probably off on some imaginary adventure of his and has forgotten all about the ribbons. Can you find out what's going on?"

"Sure thing." He walked over to the desk, nudging Jackson's boot with his own. "Hey, buddy… what are you doing?"

Jackson jerked his head up in surprise, banging it on the bottom of the desk drawer. "*Owwww…*"

Squatting down closer, Max peered in at him. "Darn, I'm sorry. I certainly didn't mean for that to happen. But what are you doing under there? Your mom needs the ribbon."

He watched as Jackson seemed to be struggling with something before he finally rolled out from under the desk. His one arm pressed to his side, as though he was hiding something, he tossed the roll of ribbon to Max. "Here, I found it."

Puzzled, Max watched as he scrambled to his feet, a guilty expression on his face. "I need to go to the bathroom. Be right back."

He ran over to the coat rack and after sending a furtive glance over at Max, he grabbed his coat and headed for the restroom.

Puzzled, Max gazed down at the roll of ribbon in his hand.

Something's up… and whatever it is, he's not planning to share. At least not yet

He picked up the box of ribbons.

He'd talk to him later.

Max handed the wrapped and tagged present to Jackson so he could add it to the already finished pile of gifts. Again, Jackson was refusing to look at him. But since he had already received a mumbled no from him when he asked if anything was wrong, he decided not to press the issue.

All of this was forgotten when Kevin and Sean came in to get some lunch. Jackson was in baseball heaven, refusing to leave their sides, peppering them with questions while they ate the pizza Crystal had ordered for all of the volunteers. By the time they went to leave, he had their promise they would come to one of his team's practice.

It wasn't until later that night he wished he would have confided in Max.

Something wasn't right.

And he wasn't quite sure what to do about it.

CHAPTER 19

*You can't start the next chapter of your life
if you keep re-reading your last one.*
~ Unknown

*M*ax had spent almost the entire day viewing one
condo after another in search for a place to live.
He had seen so many, they had all blended into one and now he
couldn't remember much about any of them.

It was already close to five when he finally told Carolyn, the
realtor assigned to him by the team's head office, he was ready
to call it a day.

He was exhausted.

He was also a little irritated.

Carolyn refused to believe he had no desire to find a place in
the city. Nor did he she understand why he didn't want to buy a
condo.

When they finally parted, with plans to meet again the next
day, he once again reminded her a house was what he wanted.
With some land... trees... and enough distance from the neighbors for privacy.

Seriously, was this too much to ask? He didn't think so.

Since you're in the public eye most of the time, you want a place to chill out. A sanctuary of sorts...

Now driving back to his hotel, he decided to stop at a little coffee shop he'd noticed earlier, Café Latte. The parking lot was still pretty full, leading him to believe it must be a popular hangout.

But this was okay. He wasn't planning on hanging around. He only wanted to pop in, order a coffee to go and zip right back out.

What you really want, more than anything, is to spend time with Jessie. But right now, this wasn't an option. She had promised Crystal she'd help out all day in the shop.

After he had his cup in hand, he headed for the door. Where he had to step aside to let two women enter.

"Max? Is that you?"

He tensed, the sound of her voice so familiar. But not in a good way. No, it was bringing back memories he knew for a fact he didn't want to remember.

He glanced over to find he was face to face with Mandy.

The same Mandy who at one time he had seriously considered asking her to marry him.

She wasn't alone. Unfortunately, she was with Margo. The same Margo from the wedding he went to with Jessie.

For a long, uncomfortable moment, they didn't speak. It was Margo, watching them with a calculating smile, who finally broke the silence.

She giggled. "Max... what a surprise. I swear it was only minutes ago I was telling Mandy about how you were at the wedding the other night. If this isn't fate, I don't know what else it could be."

She paused, tapping her finger against her lips with quite the dramatic flair. "*Hmm...* but help me out a little here. My mind has gone blank. Did you bring a date or did you come stag?"

Her comment was enough to jolt his mind back to the present. It also irritated him. So, he ignored her and turned to

Mandy, surprising himself at how casual he managed to sound. "So… it's been a while. What brings you here to Cleveland?"

She held up her hand. Her left hand, minus a ring. A hesitant smile on her face, she moved closer. "As you can see, I'm no longer engaged. I realized I'd made a big mistake. So, I've decided now might be the perfect time to re-connect with old friends, make amends."

She reached up to press a kiss to his cheek, the message in her eyes enough to make him feel very uncomfortable.

Nope, you don't want this from her. You need to get out of here. Now…

He stepped back, reaching for his keys. "I'm sorry to hear that. About the engagement, that is. But I'm sure you'll have no trouble finding someone else."

At a loss of what to say next, he sent both women a bright smile, holding up his cup. "Well, I hate to make this short, but I only came in to grab a coffee… I needed a little pick-me-up. And since I'd like to drink it while it's still hot, I better get going. Enjoy your visit here."

Giving them both a nod, he made a quick exit.

It wasn't until he was in his car and had a long drink of coffee, he finally exhaled a long sigh of relief.

Consider yourself one lucky guy. Mandy breaking up with you was the best thing that could have ever happened.

He had wondered how he would feel if he ever ran into her again. And now the verdict was in.

It was official.

He felt nothing.

In fact, Jessie was all he could think about. How much he wished he could see her right now, talk to her. Tell he what happened… how the whole time he was with Mandy, he could only think about her.

He picked up his phone and hit her number.

She answered, bringing a smile to his face. "Hey, Jess… I know you're busy, but I just wanted to hear your voice."

He closed his eyes, his voice coming out husky with longing. "I miss you."

"I miss you, too."

The smile in her voice would almost be enough to hold him over until their dinner date.

It wasn't until he got back to his hotel, he remembered he'd promised Jackson he'd come to his hockey practice.

After he called Jessie back to tell her he'd pick up Jackson from practice, he grabbed a piece of leftover pizza from the refrigerator. Wolfing down the cold pizza on the way to his car, he headed for the ice rink.

Jessie laid her phone down on the counter, a dreamy smile on her face. It was only when the customer cleared her throat, she remembered she had been in the middle of packing up a cake when Max called.

She sent the woman an embarrassed smile as she quickly put the boxed cake in a shopping bag and handed it to her. "I'm sorry. I've been here all day and it's been non-stop."

Raising an eyebrow, the woman shook her head. "Honey, there is no need to apologize. I could tell it was a man you were talking to on your phone. And the dreamy look on your face, tells me he must be pretty special."

She sent her a wink as she turned to leave. "Now you have a Merry Christmas."

After wishing her the same, Jessie gazed around at the now empty shop. Knowing this would be a good time to restock the display case, she was about to grab an empty tray when her phone rang.

It was Chad.

She dropped the still ringing phone in her pocket.

Right after that another wave of customers entered the shop.

She completely forgot about the call.

Throwing his phone down on his desk, Chad Wilson angrily strode over to the windows of his Michigan Avenue eighteenth floor office.

He was in a bad mood. In an attempt to keep from yelling at his legal assistant Gloria, he stared out the window, his gaze fixated on the blinking neon Merry Christmas sign mounted on the building across the street.

Yeah, Merry Christmas... like there was even a chance this was going to happen now.

He'd swear he had called Jessie at least a dozen times since he had arrived at the office. And every time the call went straight to her voicemail.

Did she block you?

This thought had the nervous tick in his jaw acting up. Rubbing his hand over his jaw, he let out a long, irritated sigh.

Gloria answered this with an annoyed sigh of her own. "Do you want to know what I think?"

He shrugged.

After working together for almost three years, this was something he knew was going to happen, whether he wanted it to or not. She wasn't shy about sharing her opinions.

Perched comfortably on the arm of the chair, she started right in. "Okay, maybe I shouldn't have told you about the media post? But I guess I was looking at it from my perspective. If someone found out my boyfriend was rumored to be the future fiancé of someone famous, I'd certainly want them to tell me."

Jamming his hands in his trouser pockets, he slowly turned, the intensity of his gaze immediately bringing on her look of dread.

He took a deep breath and began to speak very slowly, if only to check his anger. "The guy is not famous. He plays baseball.

Certainly not what most intelligent people would rate as a person of celebrity status."

She shrugged. "If you say so."

Sending her a sharp look, he started pacing back and forth. "And tell me, since you seem to know so much about this subject, who believes all of the nonsense written up in these articles? And more importantly, who cares?"

She was shaking her head. "You'd be surprised at the number of people who not only believe everything they read, but also care very much."

He glared at her. "You're not helping matters."

She refused to answer. Instead she watched as he continued to pace back and forth, the initial joy she had felt when she first found out about Jessie and this baseball player, now having turned to despair. She'd hoped this new development would make Chad finally realize Jessie wasn't the woman for him.

No, after working with him almost twenty-four-seven for the last three years, she... Gloria Mills, was the one who was deserving of his love.

But no... this hadn't happened.

Blinking furiously in an effort to keep back the tears, she silently slipped out of the room.

Chad hadn't even noticed she left. Signed into his computer, he was too busy checking flights to Cleveland.

It looked like he needed to work fast.

Yeah, he knew he had made a big mistake when he told Jessie they should cool it for a while. But, hey... the way he saw it, this was his only option. Everything had snowballed into such a mess, his career suddenly under scrutiny. And if one of them were to be blamed for the unfortunate mix-up with the case they ended up representing on opposite sides? It was better she was the one to take the blame, right?

He figured he'd given her enough time to cool down, think things through,

This meant it was now time for him to make his move, get

things rolling. Maybe even pop the question. This way they could start working out a plan for their future. A partnership of sorts.

Marriage was a must. This would guarantee they would always be on the same team, with him in control.

Heck, she wouldn't even have to work. Her only job would be to stand by, ready to support him and his career.

Call him old fashioned, but if he was finally to become partner, this is the way it would have to be.

Yeah, his plan was to win her trust again, bring her back to Chicago.

And what better way to do this, than to make a surprise visit.

CHAPTER 20

*M*ax entered the rink and finding a seat away from the rest of the parents, he settled into watching Jackson's practice session.

Within only a few minutes, Jackson caught sight of him, a big smile lighting up his face. Max watched as he began skating from kid to kid, pointing over to where he was sitting.

In only took a few more minutes before all eyes were on Max instead of the practice.

Not wanting to be a distraction, Max stood and yelled out, his voice carrying out over the ice. "Hey, when are we going to see some real hockey being played? That puck isn't going to get a goal by itself."

From then on, it was a competition to see who was the best on the team.

Possibly the best practice they had since the season began.

After posing for numerous photos and scribbling his autograph on almost every item imaginable, Max and Jackson were about the only ones still left in the stands.

Jackson grinned up at him. "Thanks for showing up. You

even got Andy to crack a smile. And trust me, he doesn't smile very often. Not lately, at least."

He hesitated, glancing up again at Max. "Can I ask you something?"

"Yeah, sure... ask away."

"If you think someone you know, knows about something that could get a lot of people in trouble, but you're pretty sure they had nothing to do with what happened, what would you do."

To say Max was totally confused at first by what Jackson was trying to say, would be putting it mildly. So, it was no surprise it took him a little time to come up with his answer. "I guess this would all depend if there was a chance people could get hurt because of this something?"

Jackson shook his head. "Not hurt. But they would be disappointed."

"*Ahh...* and is this person a friend of yours? Do you feel comfortable talking to them about this?" He slowly shook his head. "But no, I don't want you to even think of getting involved if there's any kind of danger. For that, you need to confide in an adult. Tell them what you know, or think you know. Let them be the one to decide what needs to be done."

Jackson took a minute to think about this. After he sent a furtive glance around the rink, he jumped up from his seat. "Wait here, I'll be right back."

He took off, running towards the locker room. When he returned he was carrying his gym bag. Plopping down next to Max, he reached into the bag and pulled out a black ski glove with green neon stripes. One of the stripes looked like it had been partially ripped off.

He handed the glove to Max. "This is Andy's glove. I know this because of the missing stripe. When we had recess at school the other day, he was wearing only one glove. I asked him why and he got all nervous like before he said he'd just lost the other one."

He stared down at the glove before he looked up at Max, a worried expression on his face. "I found this at the community center when I was trying to get that roll of ribbon out from under the desk. I knew it was his right away because of the missing stripe."

For a minute or two, they both remained silent. Then Max nodded. "I see. So, you think Andy knows something about the missing presents. But just because his glove was in the community room, doesn't mean he was involved."

"But why else would he be in the community center? I was going to give him the glove, but he's been acting so strange the last few days... not talking to anyone and going off by himself." Jackson shrugged. "So, I decided to ask you what to do."

Another silence fell between them before Max gave another nod. "If Andy is part of the reason for the missing gifts, he had to have help... or he helped someone else. There's no way he could've pulled off such a big job by himself. Also, whoever took all of the gifts had to have a van or a truck. Which means they also had to know how to drive. Andy strikes out on both counts."

His gaze traveling over to the entrance of the rink, he turned back to Jackson. "Isn't that him over by the door?"

Jackson nodded. "Yeah, that's him. He's probably waiting for someone to pick him up."

Max stood, smiling down at Jackson. "Okay, let's go over and see if he needs a ride. And you can give him the glove. But I don't want you to tell him where you found it, okay?"

Sensing Andy's apprehension when he and Jackson approached, Max kept the tone of his voice casual. "Hey, do you need a ride home?"

A relieved smile wiping away the worried expression on his face, Andy shook his head. "No, I'm sure my mom will be here any minute."

His smile quickly disappeared when Jackson pulled the glove out of his gym bag and held it out to him. "Here, I found your glove. I've been meaning to give it to you, but I kept forgetting."

Quickly stuffing the glove in his pocket and ducking his head, Andy's response was barely a mumble. "Thanks."

Max cleared his throat. "Okay then... if you're sure you have a ride, we're going to take off. We need to stop in at the community center to see if any more gifts were delivered and need to be wrapped. I'm sure you heard about the original gifts going missing. Luckily, there's a lot of generous people around and all the gifts have been replaced. Otherwise it would be a sad Christmas for a lot of kids here in town."

Andy suddenly grabbed the doorknob and pushed open the door. "I gotta go, my mom is here. Bye..."

Max called out to him. "Andy... if you need to talk, I'm willing to listen."

Coming to an abrupt stop, Andy sent Max a brief nod. Then he ran out to his mom's car and they drove away.

Massaging the back of his neck, Max looked down at Jackson. "Well... I'd say, by what we just witnessed, something fishy is going on. What it is, could be anyone's guess. Now we just need to find out if it has anything to do with the missing presents. Hopefully he'll take me up on my offer."

Jackson was worried. "Are you going to tell Captain Gunn about this?"

Visions of Bobby turning up at Andy's house, sirens blaring and lights flashing before giving him the third degree, Max slowly shook his head. "Do you know what? I don't think we will, not yet. Give me some time to think about this."

As they made their way to the car, he grinned. "Are you hungry? Because I am. I only had a piece of cold pizza for dinner. How about picking up something to take back to your house? This way I'll be able to see your Aunt Jessie, too."

"Sounds good to me." Andy shrugged. "I'm always hungry. I can eat anything, anytime."

He peered up at Max. "You really like her, don't you?"

Starting up the car, Max grinned. "Yep, just between you and me, I like her a lot."

"Mom will be happy. She's been worried Aunt Jessie is going to marry Chad. He makes her nervous, she said. Because he's too smart for his own good, whatever that means."

"*Hmm...* Chad, huh? The lawyer..."

Jason nodded, making a face. "Yeah, I don't understand... if I was Aunt Jessie, I wouldn't even have to think about it... I'd pick you."

Max laughed at this, reaching over to give him a high five. "Thanks, buddy. I appreciate your support. Now, pizza or burgers... what's it going to be?"

CHAPTER 21

The hardest thing to do is watch the one you love,
love someone else.

~ Unknown

Jackson and Crystal had gone to bed. Sharing a glass of wine with Jessie, Max had just filled her in on what happened at the ice rink.

He shrugged. "So, I told Jackson we'd keep this between us for now. Give ourselves a little time to figure it out."

Jessie responded to this with what sounded like a giggle, Surprised, Max glanced down at her. Her lips pressed together, she shook her head.

He leaned back, a smile hitching the corner of his mouth. "All right, what's going on… are you laughing at me?"

Dropping her head back against the sofa cushions, her gaze locked with his. "You can't fool me. I know how much you'd like to solve this case before Bobby does. Be the hero." She grinned up at him. "You want that home run feeling."

He laughed. "You've got that right, that's me in a nutshell. And don't you forget it."

His gaze going to the fireplace, he sighed. The fire was now almost down to a pile of embers, the flames barely a flicker. For him, this was a sign it was time for him to leave. "I think it's time for me to go. You need to get up early tomorrow and so do I."

He gathered her close, pressing a kiss in her hair. "I wish I could take you with me. Even if just for a little while. But I'm going to hold on to the promise I'll see you tomorrow night for dinner. The reservations have been made, so we're all set."

She smiled up at him. "And where will we be going?"

He shook his head. "Nope, it's a surprise. You'll have to wait until tomorrow night." After he slipped into his coat, he gave her a sweet, lingering kiss. "Until tomorrow, then?"

"Yes, tomorrow." She called out to him as he ran down the steps. "Text me when you get to your hotel so I know you're home safe."

Max had already turned on to the main highway when he realized he'd left his gloves behind. Since the realtor had promised to show him more homes with the outdoor space he'd requested, he was going to need them.

So, he turned his car around and headed back.

He arrived just in time to watch as a taxi came to a screeching halt and pulled into the driveway. A man got out and carrying a suitcase, he ran to the front door.

Max continued to watch as Jessie opened the door. The man took her into his arms and after spinning them around in circles, he gave her what appeared to be an extremely long and passionate kiss. After he sent a wave to the taxi driver, he and Jessie went inside, closing the door behind them.

At least this is what Max saw.

Was this Chad?

It had to be.

Who else would it be?

In shock, he watched the taxi drive away. Even until the tail lights were no longer visible, he remained where he was.

He was confused. His mind frantically trying to process what he just saw, his first impulse was to get out of his car and go knock on the door. Heck, he had an excuse.

He really needed his gloves.

Right?

But at the same time, he wasn't sure this was a good idea.

Do you really want to find out what's going on? Think about the kiss you just witnessed...

And just like that, his decision was made.

You are not going to let this happen...

In one quick move, he was out of the car and marching over to the front door.

When the doorbell had rung, Jessie thought it was Max, returning for his gloves. She had found them right after he left, on the floor by the coat rack. So, when she opened the door, she had the gloves in her hand and a big smile on her face. "I had a feeling you'd be back for—"

Her words came to an abrupt halt when she saw Chad. As you can imagine, he was the absolute last person she expected to see.

But before she could even question him, let alone accept he was actually standing right in front of her, he picked her up and spun her around, his mouth crashing down on hers in a long and passionate kiss.

Abruptly releasing her, he ushered them both inside and closed the door. After he removed his coat, he turned to her, a big smile on his face. "So, where do you want me to put this?"

Still in shock, she pointed to the coat rack.

His coat hung, he began rubbing his hands together for warmth. "Wow, it sure is cold out there. Must be in the single digits. I should've brought my heavier coat. But, once I was able to book a flight so quickly, I didn't have much time to think, let alone pack. I'm surprised I even brought a coat at all."

Yes, he knew he was rambling. But he was starting to get a little nervous. Her reaction wasn't quite what he'd hoped for.

Nope, she's too quiet. Which means she's thinking too hard. Yep, right now she's switched over to her lawyer mode. And you're going to be the one on trial.

He gave her what he intended as a very pitiful and endearing look. "I could really use a drink. Preferably something hot?"

Jessie's expression didn't change. If anything, she now appeared to be angry.

Very angry.

Well, he hadn't come this far to not get what he wanted. So, maybe it was time to try a different tactic?

Flashing his most enduring grin, this confirmed by almost every single one of his past girlfriends, he reached out to pull her into his arms.

He then switched over to his sexiest voice, the one up until now had never failed to work its magic. "*Come on, babe...* we both know how stubborn you can be. So, I'm willing to be the first to apologize. I certainly don't want to jeopardize what we have due to a silly misunderstanding."

She grew dangerously still in his arms.

Oh boy, not a good sign. Maybe you should've worded that a little differently?

He cleared his throat. "Of course, I'm not insinuating what happened wasn't important. And I realize it was mostly because of me the case we were on got so screwed up. But come on, babe... you know as well as I do, I'm not perfect."

Slightly pulling away from her, he gave her a big dose of his most charming smile. "Hey, neither of us are. The real test is if we can get past this and move on." His mouth brushing over hers, he pulled her even closer. "Now come on, give me a real welcome kiss..."

Her hands going to his chest, she shoved him away. She did this with such force, he almost slammed into the door.

His mouth dropping open and grabbing his arm, he stared at

her before he finally sputtered out a response. "What the...? What's got into you? You could've dislocated my shoulder..."

"Aunt Jessie?"

The sound of Jackson's voice had Jessie whirling around. He was standing at the bottom of the steps, a worried look on his face. "Are you okay? Do you want me to get mom."

She sent him a reassuring smile. "No, no... I have everything under control. There's no reason to wake up your mom?"

Crystal appeared on the steps behind Jackson. "Wake me up? Why? What's going on?"

Briefly closing her eyes, Jessie groaned. "It's nothing. Chad has now realized he made the wrong decision by coming here and once he calls for a taxi, he will be leaving."

Jackson's eyes got big. "Wow... you're Chad? He glanced over at Jessie, his whisper exaggerated. "Does Max know he's here?"

This brought an irritated, almost snorting laugh from Chad. "Yeah, Max... the infamous look-at-me-I'm-cool-I'm-a-jock-Max. A girl waiting for him in every city kind of guy. We talked about this, Jess. Don't you remember? You're the one who labeled all of these over-paid athletes as all brawn and no brains. Yeah, this Max might be able to connect the bat to a ball, but that's as far as it goes. Unless you count picking up women as one of his so-called skills. I'd be willing to bet he latched on to you as soon as he found out you're a lawyer. Probably thought he won the jack-pot... a girlfriend and someone to handle his legal work, all in one. Trust me, it won't last."

For what felt like an extremely long time, there was nothing but silence. Not even Jackson had anything to say.

Then Jessie came to life. Her fists clenched at her sides, her expression was livid. "*Get out...* I want you to leave right now. So, you can get back on a plane to Chicago and as far away from me as possible. Because, believe me, no matter what you think, there is nothing for us to talk about."

Slowly dragging his hand through his hair, he stared at her.

"What? You're actually sending me back out into the cold? But I already sent the taxi away."

But she didn't hear a single word he said. She was too busy dragging his suitcase across the floor. After she opened the door, she shoved the suitcase outside, even going as far to give it a good, hard kick.

They all watched as it rolled and bumped its way down the steps before it finally skidded off the sidewalk and plowed into a big pile of snow.

He groaned. "*Come on,* Jess. Be reasonable. I'll freeze to death out there."

She took only about a millisecond to think about this before she grabbed his coat off the coat rack and flung it out the door to land right next to his suitcase.

She turned to him. "There you go. You're all set. Now you have your coat to keep you warm." She followed this with a big smile.

But he'd be the first to tell you, it really wasn't a smile.

Oh, no... In fact, it scared him more than he'd like to admit. A worried expression on his face, he slowly began to back away.

She glared at him in return.

He swallowed, nervously.

Yeah... if she could, you have a feeling she'd send you flying right out the door after your coat and suitcase.

His eyes never leaving her face, he cautiously pulled out his phone. He punched in a number and putting the phone up to his ear, he was slowly shaking his head. "This is a side of you I've never seen before. And I have to tell ya... I don't think I like it." When she opened her mouth to respond, he held up his finger. "Hold on, they're answering."

The taxi ordered, he dropped the phone in his pocket and held up his hands in surrender. "Okay, are you satisfied? My ride is on the way. But until it gets here, I'm not going to wait outside. I'm going to wait right here. So we can talk, straighten this all out."

Crossing her arms over her chest, she shook her head. "Let me repeat what I said earlier. We have nothing... *absolutely nothing*... to talk about. Not now, not ever."

She closed her eyes. "In fact, when I open my eyes, you better be gone. Otherwise I just might do something I'll regret."

Unfortunately, he didn't heed her advice. When she opened her eyes, he was still there. So, she grabbed one of her boots from the floor and flung it right at him.

He ducked, just managing to keep it from hitting him in the head before it slammed into the door. Yanking open the door, his one hand shielding his face, he went running outside. "I'm going, I'm going..."

It was only when he was a safe distance away he finally turned back to her, his words echoing in the silence of the night. "All right... have it your way. We're done. But let it be on your conscience if I freeze to death out here."

She jerked her head towards the taxi slowly cruising up to the curb. "It must be your lucky day, because it appears that isn't going to happen. Goodbye."

She slammed the door.

Chad threw his bag in the taxi.

After almost diving in after it, he sank into the seat. Barking out his request for the airport, this was when he realized it was the same driver he had earlier.

He closed his eyes, giving a long, frustrated sigh.

Great, just great. Remember all the bragging you did? Telling him how thrilled Jessie was going to be when she saw you?

They weren't moving. He glanced over to see the driver was watching him in the rearview mirror. He was grinning.

Chad raised an eyebrow. "Yes? You have something you'd like to say?"

"Looks like it didn't work out like you planned, did it? Guess the joke is on you." He then proceeded to laugh for a good ten seconds.

The dirty look from Chad finally had him shifting the taxi in gear. He shrugged. "I get it. You're not in the mood to talk. But either way, you need to put your seatbelt on."

Resisting the urge to tell him he'd do this when he was good and ready, Chad fastened the seat belt. In an attempt to avoid any further remarks from the driver, he pulled out his phone.

He punched in a number and hit call.

"Hey... Gloria. Can you do me a favor?"

"Where are you?"

Surprisingly comforted by the sound of her voice, he almost smiled. "I'm in a taxi on my way back to the airport. It looks like Jessie and I are through. I decided we aren't right for each other after all. Naturally, she wasn't too happy. But she'll get over it."

He could see the taxi driver roll his eyes in the mirror.

After sending him a threatening look in return, he went back to his call. "I want you to call the airlines and get me the earliest flight back to Chicago. I also want you to pick me up when I get in."

He lowered his voice. "I normally wouldn't ask you to do this so late at night, but I don't think I can put up with another sarcastic, know-it-all driver."

Evidently the driver had excellent hearing, his sharp turn, on what felt like two wheels, enough to have him clinging to the armrest for dear life.

He frowned into the phone. "I've never been more serious, Gloria. I need you to pick me up. Send me a text with the info as soon as you can. Bye."

After he stuffed his phone back in his pocket, he peered over at the driver's identification tag. He was now smart enough to know it would probably be to his advantage to be nice to the guy.

Raymond was his name.

He sent him a bright smile. "So, Raymond... tell me, how long have you been in this business?"

At the same time, under the watchful eye of Jackson, Jessie was pacing back and forth, trying to calm down.

Even after Crystal came into the room and set a tray with three cups of hot chocolate on the coffee table, she continued to pace.

Crystal sighed. "Jessie... come on, sit down and have some of this hot chocolate I made. I don't know why you're so worked up about what happened. It's obvious he's not worth the effort."

Almost throwing herself on the sofa, Jessie shook her head. "I'm sorry. Truthfully, I'm angry with myself, not him. What was I thinking? What did I ever see in him? "

Crystal took a cautious sip of her hot cocoa. "Well... he is very attractive..."

At Jessie's look of disbelief, she shrugged. "Come on, Jessie... you've got to agree."

"Trust me, his good looks in no way make up for his lack of personality or the jerk he really is."

"You should forget about him and stick with Max." This coming from Jackson, Jessie laughed as she reached over to hug him. "I think you're right, Jackson."

Crystal clapped her hands together. "*Ah ha...* so you're finally ready to admit this out loud. This is good. *Really good...*"

She reached over to give Jackson a high five. "We had this one right, didn't we?"

Taking in their smiling faces, Jessie groaned. "There's no hiding anything from either of you, is there?"

She abruptly came to her feet. "But I don't think I want to talk about this anymore. If anything, I want to pretend it never even happened." She glanced over at the clock on the mantle. "I'm going to bed. It's late."

Crystal laughed. "Don't try to change the subject. And it's

only a little past ten, certainly not that late." She nodded over at Jackson. "But as far as you're concerned? It's very late. So hurry up and drink the rest of that hot chocolate"

Draining his cup in one big gulp, Jackson dragged himself off the sofa and headed for the stairs. He paused, leaning over the railing to grin at Jessie. "I like Max. He reminds me of dad. Nothing bothers him. And he really listens to what I have to say."

He turned and ran up the stairs.

Crystal smiled. "Well, there you have it. You couldn't get a better seal of approval than that. Jackson idolizes Joe."

Jessie picked up the tray and headed for the kitchen. It appeared she had nothing to say.

But she was smiling.

Max pulled into a parking space in front of his hotel.

That he had no recollection of his drive up to this point was proof of how upset he was with what he had witnessed

And, even more so, what he had heard.

He didn't understand. Jessie hadn't talked at all about Chad. The little information he had about the guy had come from either Crystal or Jackson.

Well, to be honest, you never really told her anything about Mandy. Or that you saw her with Margo.

Then again, he hadn't greeted Mandy with a kiss like Chad had given Jessie... a kiss that would fly right to the top of the charts when it came to passion.

But it was what he heard when he reached Crystal's front door that had him not only confused, but hurt.

Yes, he had heard everything Chad said.

"Yeah, Max... the infamous look-at-me-I'm-cool-I'm-a-jock Max. A girl waiting for him in every city kind of guy. We talked about this, Jess. Don't you remember? You're the one who labeled all of these over-

paid athletes as all brawn and no brains. Yeah, this Max might be able to connect the bat to a ball, but that's as far as it goes. Unless you count picking up women as one of his so-called skills. I'd be willing to bet he latched on to you as soon as he found out you're a lawyer. Probably thought he won the jackpot... a girlfriend and someone to handle his legal work, all rolled into one. Trust me, it won't last."

You can bet almost every single word Chad said was now ingrained in his mind and impossible to forget.

And what bothered him even more? Jessie hadn't denied any of it... not a single word. Nor had she defended him.

So, with no reason to stay, he turned and left.

Not once did he look back.

Now after unlocking the door to his hotel room, he dug his phone out of his pocket and threw himself on the bed. After he adjusted the pillows behind him, he stared down at the phone. He'd promised Jessie a text, but he was now unsure of what to say.

He finally typed out his message and hit send.

Safe and sound.
Hope everything's all right.
I miss you already.
See you tomorrow night.

Tossing the phone on the nightstand, he turned out the light. Clasping his hands behind his head, he stared into the darkness.

Let's just say it was a long time before he finally fell asleep.

Jessie didn't see Max's text until right before she went to bed.

She read it twice.

Hope everything's all right?

She didn't understand? What did he mean? Was there something wrong? Did he know Chad showed up unannounced?

But, how could he? He had left at least ten minutes before.

Maybe he was referring to what he told her about Jackson's friend Andy?

Yeah, this had to be it... because what else could it be?

Satisfied she now had her answer, she reached over and turned out the light. She had promised Crystal she'd help her with a big holiday order tomorrow. This meant she needed to get up early.

She fell asleep, visions of suitcases and coffee cakes dancing in her head.

CHAPTER 22

*A*ccording to the text Max sent, he was due to arrive in about ten minutes. After giving one last look in the mirror, Jessie grabbed her purse and went running downstairs.

She found Crystal in the kitchen making dinner and Jackson at the table, doing his homework. He looked up, his eyes going wide. "Wow, Aunt Jessie... you're really dressed up. Are you going to a fancy restaurant?"

Worried, Jessie glanced down at her dress before she looked over at Crystal. "Am I over-dressed?"

Crystal leaned against the sink, shaking her head. "No, you look perfect. You look like a woman who wants to look her best for her date with the man of her dreams."

In an effort to hide this had her blushing, Jessie held out her arms and turned in a circle, the skirt of her dress floating out around her. "Do you like the dress? It was my last big splurge. I fell in love with it when I saw it in the window of this little shop on Michigan Avenue. My plan had been to wear it for the firm's annual Christmas party." She made a face. "But I guess that's not going to happen, is it?"

Crystal shrugged. "It's their loss. You look beautiful. Max is going to be wowed when he sees you."

The dress was a deep emerald green brocaded satin. The bodice was fitted to her waist with a round neckline. The sleeves were three-quarter length and the skirt flared to just below her knees.

Jessie hoped Crystal was right about Max being, as she put it, wowed. But she was worried. She couldn't stop thinking about the text he'd sent last night. Or the nagging feeling something was wrong.

You would think the drive to pick up Jessie would give Max enough time to figure out how he was going to handle this new development with Chad.

But, he couldn't decide. Should he bring it up before dinner? Or would it be best to wait until after?

If he went with before, he'd have his answer right away. Everything would be out in the open. But this could also mean there would be no dinner to follow.

And if he left it until after? There would be no way he could enjoy himself, knowing what he did.

So, as you can see, he had a real dilemma on his hands.

It wasn't until he arrived at Crystal's house, he made his decision. He was going to wait until after dinner. Hopefully, this wouldn't turn out to be their one and only date.

Come on, man… chill. Everything is going to be fine.

He got out of the car, went to the front door and rang the bell.

The doorbell sent Jackson out of his chair and down the hall.

Throwing open the door, he gave Max a once over before he grinned. "Boy, it's a good thing you got all dressed up. Because wait until you see Aunt Jessie."

Max laughed. "So, she looks pretty good, huh?"

Jackson nodded.

But Max didn't see this, his attention already on Jessie as she came over to join them.

The approval in his eyes had her once again twirling around to hide that she was blushing. She gave him a shy smile. "So, what do you think?"

Catching her wrist to pull her against him, his whisper landed right below her ear. "Jess... you look beautiful." Her intention to thank him, she lifted her face to his, only to have him capture her mouth in a kiss. There was no doubt, if he could, he would have given her a much longer and even more passionate kiss, but Jackson quickly put a halt to this. "*Geeesh...* you two kiss more than anyone I know. My dad doesn't even kiss my mom this much and they're married."

Max grinned at him. "Sorry, buddy... this is what happens when you meet a beautiful woman like your Aunt Jessie. And I bet your dad kisses your mom a lot more than you know. You just don't see it all the time."

"So, where are you two headed?" This came from Crystal who had come into the room.

Max put his finger to his lips. "*Shh...* it's a surprise."

He smiled at Jessie. "Are you ready to go? We don't want to be late for our reservations."

As he drove down the street. Max glanced over at Jessie to see she was studying him, a preoccupied expression on her face.

He reached over for her hand, giving it a gentle squeeze. "Hey, why such a solemn look?"

She glanced down at their hands before she looked back at him, a faint smile on her face. "Nothing... I..."

And that plan he had? The one where he was going to wait until they were through with dinner?

This suddenly no longer felt like a good idea.

Searching for a place to park, he turned into the parking lot of the community center.

She looked surprised. "We're having dinner here?"

He shook his head and after putting the car in park, he turned to her. "No, we're not. But before we go any further, is there something you'd like to tell me?"

"I don't know… do I?" Peering over at him, she was confused. But the dark interior of the car made it hard for her to see his expression.

And this is when everything started to go all wrong… *so terribly wrong.*

Now, Max would be quick to take the blame for this. He knew his behavior was definitely out of order. But, this wasn't entirely his fault, because this is what love does to a person. The logical part of your brain suddenly bows out, leaving passion as the driving force.

And everyone knows how this can turn a person into someone completely crazy and out of control.

He gave an irritated sigh. "Come on Jess… I'm talking about last night… what happened after I left."

And now she was even more confused. After he left? What happened after he left?

Then she realized what he was talking about. She nodded, slowly. "You saw Chad. But how? I wanted to tell you about him and—"

"And what, Jess? That you realized you made a mistake by breaking up with him? I came back for my gloves and I heard everything Chad said, including your opinion of guys like me. All brawn and no brains, is what I believe you said. So, what does this mean for us? Am I only a casual fling? Someone to pass the time with during the holidays before you go back to your high profile life in Chicago?"

He shook his head. "Well… if this is what you have planned, you've picked the wrong guy."

Her silence had him diving right back in with more. Something he later wished he had never done. "But then again, maybe you're right. Remember Margo from the wedding? I ran into her and Mandy yesterday. Mandy let me know her engagement is off, hinting we should try to make a go of it again. But, this can never happen. And do you want to know why?"

Gazing down at her hands, she slowly shook her head.

His voice vibrated with emotion. "Because I thought I'd found what I wanted in you. But now? I'm not so sure."

The silence that followed seemed to drag on forever.

His head against the headrest and his eyes closed, Max was waiting for Jessie to deny what he said. Or just say something. He'd take anything... absolutely *anything*.

You should've stuck with your original plan? Instead, it now seems you've made things so much worse.

Staring blindly out the passenger window, Jessie was in shock. Yes, she had made the comment about athletes. But this had been over a year ago, when she and Chad had been discussing a case they were working on involving an abusive football player. Never, ever would she put Max in the same category.

She couldn't believe he'd think this of her. Or that he would accuse her of using him.

How had everything suddenly gone all so wrong?

Trying to hold back the tears, she closed her eyes.

Max was the first to break the silence. "Jessie, I'm sorry, I—"

She snapped, anger taking over as she turned to face him. "No, don't even say it. You've made it very clear how you feel without even giving me a chance to explain. I don't know why I feel the need to tell you this, but I literally kicked Chad out of the house. Along with his suitcase and his coat. He was in a taxi and headed back to the airport before he even knew what hit him. You can ask Crystal... or Jackson, they'll back me up on this."

And even though this was the last thing she wanted to do, she began to cry. Blindly searching for the door handle, she turned to him. "Do you know why I kicked Chad out? Because I finally realized I was in love with you... and have been from the beginning. But after what happened with him, I was afraid of getting hurt again. So I tried to deny what I was feeling."

She slowly shook her head. "What a fool I am."

She opened the car door, her words choked with tears. "Since you said you're no longer sure how you feel about me, maybe you should give Mandy a call. I'm sure she'll welcome you with open arms. And don't worry about me, I'll be fine."

He made it out of the car and over to her in record time, grabbing hold of her arm. "Jessie, stop... I'm sorry. I'm so, so sorry. Please, let's talk about this."

Without a word, she pulled her arm from his grip and began to walk away. But heels don't really do well in ice and snow.

After two near falls, Max groaned, grabbing hold of her arm again. "Jess, come on. No matter how you feel about me right now, at least let me take you home. I'll never forgive myself if you fall and get hurt."

She came to a sudden halt, giving him hope. But this disappeared when she barely even glanced at him as she pulled her phone out of her coat pocket. "It's Crystal. I have to answer because it could be about the baby."

After she ended the call, she still refused to meet his gaze. "Andy showed up at the house. Crystal said he's all worked up about something, but won't say what it is. He told her he can only talk to you. He said it's important."

Relieved, he reached for her hand. When he realized she was shaking, he quickly removed his overcoat and draped it over her shoulders before leading her back to the car. "Come on, let's get you back in the car where it's warm. I promise you needn't talk or even look at me."

And this is exactly what she did.

Her face turned to the window, she didn't utter a single word.

So, it was a very silent drive home.

But he was okay with this. He needed all the time he could get.

If only to give him a chance to make things right.

Jessie was sitting at the kitchen table, her hands wrapped around the mug of hot tea Crystal had made for her.

She couldn't seem to get warm. Even with Max's overcoat draped over her shoulders, she was still shaking.

She was aware of the worried glances Crystal and Jackson kept sending each other. And she knew they were waiting for her to tell them what happened.

But she couldn't... not yet.

You're not even sure yourself what happened. Only that everything is a mess.

The low murmur of voices coming from the living room finally came to a stop. When Max walked into the kitchen, Crystal and Jackson both looked over at him, hoping for an explanation.

Unfortunately, the one person he cared about the most? Staring into her cup, Jessie refused to meet his gaze.

Hiding his disappointment, he turned to Crystal and Jackson. "Andy and I have to meet with Captain Gunn. If everything goes as planned, whoever stole the gifts could be in custody tonight. Thanks in a big part to Andy."

His mouth twisted in a wry smile. "It looks like their downfall was due to their greediness. And following Captain Gunn's orders, this is the only information I can give you right now. But I don't think it matters, because even if I told you what I know, you wouldn't believe me."

He glanced over at Jessie, a sadness creeping into his voice. "Hopefully, you'll welcome me back."

Crystal sighed. "Of course, we will. Anytime. Please, if it's not too late, stop by and let us know what happened."

After a slight hesitation, he leaned down to press a kiss to Jessie's cheek. "Again, I'm so sorry about how this evening has gone. I'll make it up to you, I promise."

When she didn't respond, he sent Jackson and Crystal a brief smile and left.

For a minute or two, the ticking of the old antique clock on top of the refrigerator was the only sound in the room. Finally, Crystal glanced over at Jackson.

He shrugged. "So, now what do we do?"

"You need to go to bed."

Glancing over at the clock, he started to laugh. "Mom, it's only seven-thirty."

"Oh, so it is. It seems much later. Too much excitement, I guess. Well, go take a shower. Go on, you might as well get it over with."

He sighed... loudly. "Ok, but I'm staying up in case Max comes back. No matter how late it is."

"We'll see. Now, go. And wash up good, your hair, too. It's starting to look a little scraggly."

As soon as he disappeared up the stairs, Crystal moved over to sit next to Jessie. "Jess, honey, what happened?"

Jessie's tears started up all over again as she told her about Max's accusations.

When she was finished, Crystal sighed. "Falling in love is so crazy sometimes. Your emotions are so fragile and you tend to do and say things you don't mean."

Her head down on her arms, Jessie let out a big trembling sigh. "He was so angry, he wouldn't even give me a chance to say anything."

"He was probably scared."

Jessie lifted her head to look at her. "Scared?"

Crystal nodded. "Yes, afraid he's going to lose you. Jess, again... the man is so in love with you. It shows on his face whenever he looks at you."

"I don't know... after what happened tonight, maybe that's no longer true." She smiled wistfully over at Crystal. "I'm so in love with him, too. As soon as I saw him tonight, all I could think about was how much I wanted to tell him this. When he asked me if something was bothering me, I almost did. But then I panicked, afraid of what he'd say. And now I wish I had just blurted it out."

She reached for a tissue from the box Crystal had set in front of her and wiped the tears from her face. "I don't want to see him if he comes back tonight. I need to think about what I want to say to him."

She stood, sending Max's overcoat off her shoulders and sliding to the floor. She stared down at it before she glanced over at Crystal.

Her face crumpling, she started to cry again. "Oh no... not only is he missing his gloves, now he doesn't even have his coat."

Crystal put her hands on her shoulders and gave her a little push towards the stairs. "Go upstairs and go to bed or whatever. Tomorrow is a new day. I have a feeling the two of you will work it all out."

After she put their cups in the dishwasher, Crystal closed her eyes, massaging her aching back.

She was so tired of being pregnant. And she missed Joe.

So much...

As she went to shut off the light, she glanced out the kitchen window. A few random stars were peeking out between the clouds.

She closed her eyes and made a wish. Then she cheated a little... she made another one. The way she saw it, there was a good chance they could come true.

After all, it was Christmas.

A time for miracles...

Andy hadn't said a word since they got into Max's car. Staring straight ahead, he looked like he was about to be sick. Or cry.

Possibly even both and at the same time.

Max turned into Jed's auto repair lot and parked near the back as Bobby had advised. He could see two police cars hidden among the other cars in the lot.

When he had called Bobby to let him know Andy had information there could be another theft taking place at the community center within the next hour, this was where Bobby instructed him to come. He claimed it offered a perfect view of the community center.

He was right.

He also reminded Max, more than once, he and Andy needed to remain as inconspicuous as possible.

Before they got out of the car, Max turned to Andy. "You do know you're doing the right thing, don't you?"

Andy nodded. "Yeah, but will I get into trouble for telling on them? My Uncle Marcus told me they were moving the gifts to a more secure place. I didn't know they were stealing them. Honest, I didn't."

Max slowly shook his head. "I'd say there's a ninety-nine percent chance you won't get into trouble. You were only following your uncle's orders."

He smiled. "And you did, as they say in the movies, spill the beans. Something I know must have been hard for you."

More than happy to see he'd managed to get at least a little smile from Andy, he gave his knee a reassuring pat. "Come on, let's go talk to Captain Gunn so you can tell him what you know. I have a feeling he is going to have a lot to say."

On the contrary?

Bobby had very little to say.

Unless you want to count the low and barely audible string of curse words coming from him as he paced back and forth.

It was obvious he was having a very difficult time taking in what Andy had to tell him.

Max finally spoke. "I know you're finding this hard to believe. I did, too. And I don't even know these people as well as you do. But if what Andy is telling us is true, something should be happening any moment. Then you'll have all the proof you need."

He sent a glance over at the community center. "Speak of the devil, look... there's a truck pulling up to the entrance right now."

Bobby, or Captain Gunn as he had already once reminded Max, was on his phone in a flash. "George, your superior here. You know the drill. Get a video of everything, because we need all the evidence we can get. But make sure you stay out of sight. When you see they're almost done loading the truck, contact me. We'll be right there to cut off any chance of a getaway."

He was quiet for a few moments before he nodded. "Okay, only two suspects is great news. I'll be waiting for your call."

Once he slipped the phone in his pocket, he glanced over at Max.

He shook his head. "You're right, I am having a hard time. I don't understand... is it the money? Or the thrill of getting away with something? And then, to come back a second time?"

He shook his head again. "It just goes to show... you think you know someone and then something like this happens. Go figure..."

He reached over to squeeze Andy's shoulder. "I want to thank you for doing the right thing by confiding in an adult. And don't worry, no one needs to know about your involvement. We'll keep this between us." He nodded. "I'd say you have the makings of becoming a stellar police officer or detective in the future."

"*Wow*, do you think so? Thanks."

When Bobby gave him a thumbs up, the relief on Andy's face was visible even in the darkness.

Bobby's phone rang. He whipped it out of his pocket and put it up to his ear. "We're on our way."

Taking off for his car, he glanced back at Max and Andy. "You two go home. I don't think we're going to have any trouble, but I don't want to take any chances. If I need to talk to either of you, I'll be in touch."

Max and Andy watched the two police cars go tearing out of the lot and head for the community center.

After they pulled up behind the truck, their sirens on and lights flashing, Max put his hand on Andy's shoulder. "Come on, I'll take you home. I hope you didn't take off without telling your mom where you were going?"

The look of guilt on Andy's face gave Max his answer.

"Well, you need to tell her what happened. If you'd like, I'll come with you and let her know Captain Gunn said there's no reason for anyone to know you were involved. Okay? But whatever happens, I know she's going to be very proud of you."

His shoulders slumping in relief, Andy nodded.

On the drive to Andy's house, Max kept the conversation lighthearted. They talked sports and when it came to baseball, Max found Andy had just as many, if not more, questions about the game than Jackson did.

He hadn't thought this would be possible.

When Max finally left Andy's house, according to his watch, it was only eight-thirty. He'd swear it felt more like midnight.

He glanced down at his suit. What was it they said? All dressed up and no place to go?

Well, this description fits you perfectly, doesn't it?

To top it off, not only was he missing his gloves, he now also had no coat. And it was cold... really cold. It was a relief when the heat finally began to come on in his car.

At the end of Andy's street, he paused at the stop sign.

A right turn would have him headed in the direction of Crystal's house.

He could use the excuse he wanted to pick up his gloves and overcoat... or give a report of what happened with Andy.

A left turn would send him towards his hotel.

He turned left. Even though this wasn't what he wanted to do.

Give him a break... he was trying to be sensible about this. Something it appeared he hadn't been up until now.

He and Jessie needed time to think... calm down. Obviously, this advice would apply more to him than it would to her

He already had a plan in place. He was going to stop by the shop tomorrow and ask her if they could talk. Whenever and wherever she wanted. He didn't care. And he wasn't going to leave until she agreed to this.

In the meantime, he was going to hold on to the one bit of hope he had tucked away in not only his head, but in his heart.

She said she had fallen in love with him.

For now? This was enough.

Captain Gunn was sitting at his desk. Usually he liked to put his feet up at this late time of day. But this wasn't what he'd consider a typical day at the station. He still couldn't quite believe what just happened only about an hour ago.

Did you dream this? But then maybe dream would be a bad choice of words. This is more like your worst nightmare.

The sound of someone blowing their nose had him glancing over at the chair in front of his desk. Her head bowed and a whole pile of used tissues on her lap, Robin had been sitting in his office for the last half hour or so, sobbing uncontrollably. And now she was finally silent.

Thank the lord for that.

He cleared his throat. "Robin, look at me."

She shook her head.

He sighed. "Come on... it's me, Bobby. Just look at me."

This had her starting to cry all over again. "It's Captain Gunn, remember? You'll probably never be Bobby to me again. Not after I go down on record in Blossom Falls as the notorious Christmas gift thief and spend the next twenty years in jail."

He sighed again. He had always known she was an emotional kind of woman, but he credited this to her theatrical talent. Not that he'd ever seen her on stage anywhere. But if she claimed she had talent, who was he to disagree?

"Robin, you probably won't wind up in jail." This is when he decided maybe it was time to try for a little humor... lighten things up a little. He chuckled. "At least not for twenty years."

This brought on an even louder wail as she reached for another tissue.

Oh, boy... that was a really bad move on your part.

Shaking his head, he leaned forward. "Robin, come on... stop crying and look at me."

She shook her head. So, he used his tough cop voice, the one he practiced when he was alone. "Robin, I want you to look at me and I want you to do this right now."

He was pleased to see this worked when she lifted her head to gaze mournfully at him.

She was a wreck. Her mascara was in streaks down her face, her nose was a bright red and after running her hands constantly through her hair, because of the enormous volume of hairspray she used, it was sticking out in all directions. There was no doubt in his mind, if she had even a clue of what she looked like, this would set her off again. Maybe even enough to have her lose it completely.

He shook his head. "I want to know one thing and this is... what the heck were you thinking?"

She blew her nose, shaking her head. "I already told you. I needed the money." She sighed, long and dramatically. "Since the divorce, I never seem to have enough money to make through the month." She gazed at him with mournful eyes. "Do you know how expensive food is? And every day it seems like there are even more bills in the mailbox. Lately, I haven't even opened most of them… I just throw them away."

Trying not to show his shock at this, he cleared his throat and clasping his hands together on the desk, he nodded. "Okay… that might not be a good idea. But we'll worry about that later. What I want to know, if you needed help, why didn't you come to me?"

Her head jerked up. "You would have given me money?"

He frowned. "Well, maybe give isn't the right word to use. More like a loan? But, either way, I would have helped you, no questions asked." He shrugged. "For you, I'd do anything."

As soon as these words came out of his mouth, he slowly sat back in his chair. Massaging the back of his neck, he stared at the Norman Rockwell policeman print hanging on the wall.

He'd swear, it was like a lightbulb went off in his head. What he just said? He had meant every word. Because even though Robin irritated him at times, there was something about her that made him feel like he was the strongest, smartest and bravest man in the world.

Well, maybe not the world, but at least here in Blossom Falls.

So, when she lifted her head and looked right into his eyes, he gave her more than a reassuring smile. "We'll figure this out, Birdy. Don't you worry."

Birdy… this is the nickname he'd given her when they were in junior high. That this had popped out of his mouth now, surprised him as much as it did her.

A knock on the door to his office had him sitting up straight in his chair and slipping back into Captain Gunn, ready for business as usual.

"Come in."

Robin wouldn't be able to tell you what happened after that. This was because she couldn't stop thinking about the message she was pretty sure she saw in Bobby's eyes.

She was beginning to think there might be hope for her after all.

CHAPTER 23

Welcome to our world, little one.
As far as Christmas gifts go, you're the best.
~ Anonymously Yours

*C*rystal put the last tray of cakes in the display case under the watchful eyes of a little girl who had her face pressed against the glass.

She sighed. Any other day, this wouldn't bother her. She'd think it was cute. But, today? Her only thought was now this meant she was going to have to clean the glass all over again.

She woke up in a bad mood and she was still cranky. Maybe now even crankier, if there was such a word. And now it wasn't even mid-afternoon and she was ready to go home.

Massaging her aching back, she glanced over at Jessie. Leaning against the counter, she was staring down at her phone. Then she frowned and snatching the phone from the counter, she dropped it in her pocket.

Crystal joined her, leaning on the counter next to her.

"Hey, are you all right? For a minute there, it looked like you were going to throw your phone right out the window."

Avoiding her gaze, Jessie gave a curt nod. "Yeah, I'm fine.

Thinking about how I still don't have all of my Christmas shopping done and Christmas is only a couple days away."

"Don't worry about it... except for Jackson. At his age, it's all about the presents, unfortunately."

Jessie smiled. "I have his gift already." She frowned. "At the time, I thought signing him up for the Cleveland kid's baseball camp was a good idea, but now..."

Crystal gave her a reassuring smile. "I can assure you, he will be thrilled. He always likes your gifts." She hesitated. "Did you get a gift for Max?"

Jessie was saved from answering this when the door flew open and Susan came running into the shop. She was waving her phone in the air, immediately catching everyone's attention.

She was out of breath, hardly able to get out the words. *"Oh my, oh my, oh my...* have you seen the latest post on The Register Police Blotter page on social media?"

She handed her phone to Crystal. With Jessie leaning over her shoulder to follow along, Crystal read it aloud.

The Register Police Blotter of Blossom Falls -
  Where Justice is Always Served
  Tuesday, December 22.

  After receiving an anonymous tip at approximately eight-nineteen last evening, two suspects were sighted driving a large un-marked van out of the community center parking lot. They were immediately apprehended and the van was searched.

  The inspection confirmed the two suspects had been in the process of stealing the gifts recently donated for the Christmas Toys and Tots Annual Christmas Drive.

  Robin Miller, age thirty-one, who was driving the van and her accomplice Marcus Robertson, age forty-two, were both charged with two counts each of breaking and entering and grand theft. The double charges stem from the belief both Miller and Robertson are also responsible for the prior theft of gifts from the community center a little over a week ago.

When first questioned, Miller claimed she was innocent. She later broke down, admitting any money made from selling the gifts on-line would go toward the outstanding bills accrued because of her divorce.

After spending the night in jail, both Miller and Robertson posted bond and were allowed to return home.

A court date has yet to be set.

At first, there was complete silence.

Then the room erupted into complete chaos.

This news was shocking... unthinkable. One of their own had done this despicable act? Susan could only watch as her phone was passed from person to person so they could read the post for themselves.

Even after this, the news was still almost too hard to comprehend.

Gazing around at all of the bewildered faces, Jessie suddenly started to giggle. Swiftly turning to her, Crystal hissed. "*Stop it... just stop it.*"

Putting her hand over her mouth and shaking her head, Jessie went sprinting into the back room.

When Crystal joined her, Jessie held her hands up in surrender. She was still laughing "I'm sorry. I have no idea what's wrong with me. Maybe it's thinking of all the grief she's given us over the years. Or the snobbish act she puts on all the time. Whatever it is, I suddenly found the whole situation so funny."

"And at the same time, extremely sad." Giving a huge sigh, Crystal began assembling one of the cake boxes stacked on the table. "Poor Andy. Thank goodness, even though Marcus is his uncle, he was smart enough to confide in Max. But I wonder what big promises this Marcus gave Robin, persuading her to go along with his plan?"

Jessie slowly shook her head. "Who knows? It's amazing what people will do for money. Even the short time I've been a lawyer, I could tell you so many stories. I'm sure Andy feels so relieved now, knowing he did the right thing."

When Crystal had no comment, Jessie glanced over just in time to see a surprised look flash across her face before she placed her hands on her stomach. Then she closed her eyes, her face screwing up in pain.

She sent Jessie a tentative smile. "Oh, boy... I was hoping I'd make it through the afternoon, but I do believe it may be time to head for the hospital. I've been feeling contractions all morning, but now they're getting a lot stronger and closer together."

Jessie immediately went into a panic, removing her apron with shaking hands. "Oh my gosh... why didn't you say something? What should we be doing? Timing the contractions? Do you need to go home first? I know you have a bag packed and ready to go right by the front door."

A look of absolute horror came over her face. "You're not going to have the baby here, are you?"

Crystal started to laugh, this ending with another grimace. She took a deep breath. "Calm down, everything is going to be fine. We've got plenty of time." She shook her head. "This is exactly why I didn't say anything earlier. I knew you would react this way."

She glanced over at the crowded shop, now the unofficial gathering place to discuss the latest news about the break-in.

She groaned. "*Oh, no...* doesn't this figure. The place is packed. I want you to go tell Marilyn we're leaving and she's in charge. Her niece is here, so she should be fine."

When she saw Jessie was rooted to the spot, staring at her, she waved her hand in front of her face. "Jess, come on... get a move on. But make sure when you tell Marilyn, you keep it low key."

Jessie went flying into the shop, where Crystal watched her whisper into Marilyn's ear. Any possibility of keeping their departure quiet immediately disappeared when Marilyn enfolded Jessie in a big hug, letting out a loud shriek. "Oh my gosh, everybody... the baby's coming."

Crystal could only watch as the crowd flowed into the back

room, everyone showering her with wishes for good luck, giving her advice and nearly smothering her with hugs. Searching the room for Jessie, she finally saw her waving by the door.

They were finally in Jessie's SUV, shouts of encouragement still coming from the crowd gathered outside.

Unfortunately, they weren't moving.

Crystal glanced over at Jessie. Mumbling to herself, she was frantically searching for her keys.

Crystal sighed, pointing at the keys in the ignition... where Jessie had already put them. After starting up the SUV, Jessie sent her an embarrassed grin. "Sorry, you should be the crazy one, not me. But don't worry, I'll be fine once we get going."

But this became questionable when she stepped on the gas to send them shooting out onto the main road. Clutching the arm rest, Crystal sent her a wary glance. "*Hmm... are you sure you're fine? Because you took that a little too fast, wouldn't you say?"*

When Jessie ignored this, she sighed. "I hope you settle down by the time we get to the hospital. Otherwise, you're not going to be much help in the delivery room."

Jessie almost swerved off the road. "Again, sorry about that... but you want me in the delivery room?"

"Of course, I want you there. I've already let the hospital know you'll be taking Joe's place."

Jessie let this sink in before she spoke. "What about Jackson? No one will be there when he comes home from school."

"That has already been taken care of. I called Max."

Again, Jessie almost drove off the road, this time just barely missing a mailbox. Flustered, she glanced over at Crystal. "Again, sorry. But Max? Why Max?"

Crystal shrugged. "Because I knew I could count on him to be there for me. He told me he already feels like he's family."

After watching what she was pretty sure was a smile flash across Jessie's face, she continued. "About an hour ago, I knew things were starting to happen. So, I called him and asked if he could pick up Jackson from school and bring him to the hospital. He didn't even hesitate. He said he'd be honored to help out. He also wanted to make sure you'd be okay with this."

Holding on to the armrest for dear life as Jessie made a sharp turn into their driveway, she sent her a sly grin. "I told him I was pretty sure you'd be more than okay."

Her face suddenly twisting into a grimace, she closed her eyes for a few seconds before she took another deep breath. "I probably shouldn't tell you this, but I have a feeling this baby is in a bit of a hurry to come into the world."

This was enough to send Jessie sprinting for the house to get her bag.

Watching her trip and almost wipe out on the steps, Crystal shook her head.

Why did people act so crazy when they fell in love?

She tried to think back... had she and Joe been like that?

Watching as Jessie came running back down the driveway, bag in hand, she grinned.

It looked like this was going to be an interesting Christmas.

Jessie waited until the monitor showed the latest contraction was over before she slowly eased her hand from Crystal's iron like grip.

After she gave her hand a good shake, hoping to bring back some of the feeling in her fingers, she gave Crystal a big smile. "It looks like the nurse was right... it's not going to be much longer."

An exhausted smile on her face, Crystal closed her eyes. "Well, bring it on. Because I am more than ready."

He lashes fluttering open, she gazed over at Jessie. "I'm so glad you're here. It's not the same without Joe, but you've been great. Thank you."

"You're more than welcome." Patting her hand, Jessie

grinned. "So, does this mean if it's a girl, you're going to name her after me?"

"We'll see..." Crystal was just barely able to answer this before another contraction hit.

It appeared both Crystal and the nurse had called it right.

This baby was more than ready to come into the world.

Welcome, Amelia Jessica McDonnell
Born on December 22 at 3:45 pm
7 pounds, 4 ounces
21 inches
Parents ~ Crystal and Captain Joseph McDonnell USA
Big Brother ~ Jackson

Both mother and baby are doing just fine.
More than fine...

CHAPTER 24

*I*n awe, Jessie gazed down at the perfect little bundle in her arms that was Amelia. Adjusting the receiving blanket more securely around her, she smiled when her face scrunched up in protest at this move.

She glanced over at Crystal. Propped up against the pillows, with Jackson snuggled up beside her, she smiled. "So, what do you think?"

"Oh, Crystal… she's beautiful." Jessie grinned. "And, of course, I love the names you chose, especially the middle name."

"Amelia was our mom's name." Crystal directed this information to Max. Leaning against the wall, he was watching Jessie with the baby.

He smiled. "It's a beautiful name. But, to be truthful, I'm more partial to the middle name." Hoping this would bring at least some kind of response from Jessie, even a little smile, he gave a disappointed sigh when she remained silent, focused on the little pink bundle in her arms.

Max glanced over at Crystal.

Her eyebrows raised, she shrugged.

Jessie suddenly looked up. "Max, would you like to hold her?"

"Me?"

He looked so surprised, she couldn't help it, she laughed. "Yes, you."

She stood, handing Amelia to him. This brought such a look of panic to his face, she gestured to the chair. "You can sit down if this would make you feel more comfortable."

But after gazing down at the baby in his arms, he began walking slowly around the room. Gently rocking Amelia in his arms, he began murmuring softly to her.

Watching this, Jessie wanted to cry. Blinking like crazy, she stared up at the ceiling.

She was having a really hard time. When he and Jackson had finally been allowed to come into the room, she had wanted to run right into his arms.

Instead, she made a big fuss over Jackson when he held Amelia for the first time. At least this gave her an excuse for her emotional state.

She was a mess. She didn't want to be mad at Max. And she didn't want him to be mad at her. Nor did she want to fight with him. She only wanted to know why he had become so angry with her. And why he hadn't given her the chance to explain.

She was also hurt he hadn't trusted her enough to know what he'd accused her of? This was something she would never do.

No, you love him too much.

Caught up in her thoughts, she was unaware he had come to stand next to her. He cleared his throat. "Jess?"

His gaze locked with hers. And for the longest time they didn't move, they didn't speak. Once again, he had fallen right into the magic of her eyes. It was only when Amelia suddenly gave a little squeak, he blinked.

He pressed a soft kiss to Jessie's forehead, his eyes searching hers, his voice low. "I don't think I ever told you, the first thing I noticed about you was your eyes. They aren't only blue, they're made up of so many shades of blue, changing with your every emotion, letting me know what you're thinking. And I get lost in them every time, Jess... *every single time.* They're the only eyes I want to look into for the rest of my life."

Now this is when, if they were anywhere else, he would have given her a kiss to let her know he meant every word he said.

Instead, he gazed down at Amelia before he gave a long, resigned sigh. "There is so much more I want to say, but not now. This time belongs to you and your family in celebration of this amazing little bundle I'm holding in my arms."

Jessie closed her eyes. Now she was to the point she wanted to put her head on his shoulder and bawl her eyes out.

Why did he always have to say such nice things? Making you love him even more? You don't have a chance...

She took in a deep breath and gazing back up at him, she nodded. "Later, then?"

Let's face it, you'll agree to anything if it's with him...

Encouraged by her response, Max pressed the lightest of kisses to her cheek. "Later... for sure."

He was smiling as he took Amelia and gently placed her in Crystal's arms. "She's beautiful, Crystal."

Then he grinned over at Jackson. "And I have a feeling you're going to be the best big brother."

Half asleep, Jackson gave him a lazy grin.

Max reached for his coat. "I'm going to take off."

Crystal nodded, a thoughtful look on her face. Enough to make him pause, wondering if there was something she wanted to ask him.

There was. She smiled at him. "What are your plans for Christmas? Are you going to spend it with your family?"

He hesitated, sending a brief glance over at Jessie. "I'm not sure. I guess it depends on a few things. I've narrowed down my home search, but there are still a few details I need to work out." A wry smile his face, he shook his head. "Hotel living is getting old."

Jamming his hands in his pockets, he shrugged. "So, I guess

my plans are pretty flexible." This was followed by another glance over at Jessie.

Picking up on this, Crystal nodded.

When honestly? She seriously wanted to scream.

If she could, she'd sit the two of them down and order them to stay right where they were until they worked things out. She had a feeling once they did this, everything would fall into place. And as much as she knew this wasn't any of her business, she wanted this to happen right here in Blossom Falls. Or somewhere close by could also work. She was more than willing to compromise.

But not too much…

But this would have to wait until later. Right now, it looked like Jessie and Max needed a little help if they were going to get this right.

So, she sent Max a big smile. "I see… Well, if you do decide to stay, you are more than welcome to spend both Christmas Eve and Christmas Day with us. It won't be fancy, and probably pretty hectic, but we'd love to have you."

Once again, Max glanced over at Jessie. He wanted a sign from her she agreed with Crystal's invitation. Her slight nod, along with the briefest of smiles flitting across her face, was good enough for him.

So, he was smiling when he turned back to Crystal. "Sure, I'd like that. And if you need anything, groceries, running errands or," here he grinned, "diapers? Let me know. I'll get on it."

"Max?"

He was almost out the door when Jessie's hesitant summons had him eagerly turning around. "Yes?"

Her arms wrapped around herself, she averted her gaze as she spoke. "The night before Christmas Eve, tomorrow night, is when they hand out the gifts at the community center. It's always been a big thing here in town. Just about everyone shows up, if even for a little while."

Glancing over at Crystal, who nodded in agreement, she

continued. "It's like an old-fashioned pot luck dinner, everyone brings their favorite dish, Blossom Falls brings out their famous Christmas punch and of course, Santa makes an appearance. They even bring in a band for dancing."

She shrugged. "It's a local band, but they're not that bad."

He smiled. "Sounds like a lot of fun."

She nodded. "It is. And this year, I think you should make an appearance. After all, you've done so much to help out with the gifts and everything. And I know everyone would be thrilled to meet you... especially the kids."

For the longest time he didn't say anything, making her wonder if he was trying to think up an excuse. It was when she was about to tell him not to worry, it was only a suggestion, he slowly strolled over to stand next to her. Gently tucking her hair behind her ear, she could see the hint of a smile on his lips. "Thrilled, huh? You think so? I'm finding it hard to believe anyone is thrilled with me right now. Especially the one person I care about the most. But, I'm not yet ready to give up hope. So, I'll be more than happy to make an appearance. But only under one condition... and this is you'll come with me."

Again, she was hit by this sudden urge to burst into tears. This came at her so quickly, she was lucky she could even manage a nod.

The conflicting emotions swirling in her eyes had him reaching over to stroke her cheek, his voice rough with emotion. "Good... maybe I'll even be able to persuade you to share a dance with me?"

He frowned. "Unless it's a polka. Please don't tell me they play only polkas. My Great Aunt Ellen spoiled that dance for me forever."

She laughed, a shaky laugh. "Come on, give the people of Blossom Falls some credit. Just because this isn't the big city, doesn't mean they don't keep up with the times."

Giving her another smile, he slowly began backing away. "Okay, it's a date." Her swift glance had him clearing his throat, jumping in to reassure her. "Sorry... outing, I meant to say outing. Or whatever you want to call it. I'll pick you up around seven-thirty."

Almost as if he was afraid she'd suddenly change her mind, he turned and swiftly left the room.

Slowly sinking down into the chair, Jessie gazed over at Crystal. She opened her mouth, to then close it before she slowly shook her head.

Crystal sighed. "Jessica Louise Carter... if you don't see it, I don't know what's wrong with you. Because if that wasn't an exchange between two people who are so deeply in love with each other, I don't know what it was."

She gazed down at Amelia in her arms. Tracing her tiny mouth with her fingertip, she smiled. "Sweet little Amelia, I sincerely hope you'll be a lot smarter than your Aunt Jessie when you finally fall in love with someone."

She sighed. "That is if daddy even lets you get near a boy to have this happen...

CHAPTER 25

Dear Santa,
Before I explain…
how much do you already know?
~ Anonymously Yours

*M*ax tossed the pen on the desk and leaned back in his chair. He was smiling as he watched Carolyn gather up the mountain of papers and stack them into a neat pile.

She gazed over at him, sending him a huge smile. "That's it, everything is signed and notarized. Since I know you want the transfer to go through as quickly as possible, I will do my best to make this happen."

He nodded. "Great. And now I have a big favor to ask of you."

Shoving the papers in her briefcase, her mind already on what was next on her agenda, she almost groaned aloud. She had Christmas shopping to finish, and glancing down at her watch, she saw it was already pushing six.

But, the professional she was, she knew she had an obligation to see this deal through to the end. After all, the commission she earned from the sale would be more than enough to pay for all of the gifts she intended to buy.

Clasping her hands together in front of her, she gave him another smile, this one even brighter. "Sure... what's on your mind?"

"There's something I'd like to do before Christmas. But in order to pull it off, I'll need your help."

She frowned, gazing at him over the rims of her glasses. "Max, you do know Christmas is in two days."

"I know." Giving her his most charming smile, he shrugged. "But this is something that involves my future and if anyone can help me, it's you. Think of it as a way to make our deal even more spectacular. And after you've found the exact type of property I was looking for? I promise I'll be more than happy to recommend your services."

She laughed. "Okay, okay... enough of the flattery. But now you have me a little worried about this favor of yours, whether it's even doable."

He nodded. "It might be a little unconventional, even for you. I'd like you to put a hold on to this contact until tomorrow night."

For a moment she had no reaction. At least on the outside. Inside, everything was gearing up in protest. Then she cleared her throat. "May I again remind you it's only two days until Christmas, with tomorrow Christmas Eve?"

He chuckled. "Yes, I am very aware of this. Let me tell you my reason for doing this..."

Max was running late.

His special request to Carolyn had materialized much quicker than either of them had anticipated, her call coming right after he left his hotel to pick up Jessie. This had him making an unplanned stop at her condo to pick up the envelope she left under her front door mat. Then he had to deal with the heavier than usual traffic because of all the last-minute Christmas shoppers.

So, by the time he pulled up Crystal's driveway, he was almost fifteen minutes late.

When Jessie opened the door, without mentioning his detour to Carolyn's condo, he began rambling on and on about why he was late. "I should have called. I don't know what I was thinking. I'm sorry..." His words fading into silence, he shrugged.

Come on, the way you're acting, you'd think you were nervous about something.

Well, maybe this is because he was. There was a lot he wanted to say and he was worried he was going to goof it up. As of late, his track record hadn't been the best, so the odds this could happen were pretty high.

More relieved than anything he'd finally arrived, Jessie smiled, briefly putting her hand on his arm. "It's okay. It won't be a big deal if we're a little late. This is a very casual event, the goal to have fun and celebrate Christmas. It's all about giving a little dose of cheer to the families who need it most right now."

Even through the sleeve of his flannel shirt, her touch had been electric. This had him moving closer, the intensity of his gaze sending her heart beating into overdrive.

And now she was the one who was nervous. When a loud beeping pierced the silence, she almost took off in a run to the kitchen.

Following her, Max watched her pull a pan out of the oven, a delicious aroma wafting through the kitchen. He leaned against the counter and took in a deep breath. *"Ahh...* smells heavenly. Please tell me it's Crystal's lasagna?"

She nodded as she turned off the oven. Then she set the potholder on the counter, trying to ignore how close he was, his shoulder brushing against hers.

Her senses sent whirling, it was almost too much. Almost to the point she couldn't think.

He asked you about lasagna... you should be able to come up with an answer to that...

She sent him a brief smile. "Yes, it is. She made it a few days ago and put it in the freezer. It's a good thing she called this morning reminding me to put it in the oven." She sent him a guilty look. "I almost forgot."

She certainly wasn't going to tell him this was because she'd spent so much time trying to decide what to wear for tonight. But she wanted to look good... *really* good. She wanted to get that knocked-his-socks-off kind of look from him.

The exact kind of reaction Crystal was always carrying on about.

As if he read her mind, he moved even closer. Lightly tracing the neckline of her cashmere sweater with his fingertip, the huskiness of his whisper messed with her senses all the more. "You look so pretty, Jess. I don't know what's sparkling more... the gems on your sweater or your beautiful eyes."

He cupped her chin in his hand, turning her face to his. "*Hmm...* let me see."

After what felt like forever, his gaze roaming in an almost agonizing slow journey over her face, he nodded. "I'd have to go with your eyes, hands down. Of all the things I love about you, they're what I fell in love with first."

Her head jerking up, she searched his face.

Love?

Immediately flustered, she ducked down and began searching through one of the bottom cupboards. She was looking for what Crystal used to transport the hot dishes she made for this kind of event. She called them casserole cozies? She swore they were a godsend, kept a dish hot for hours.

She finally found what she was looking for in the far corner, tucked behind a stack of tablecloths. This meant she almost had to crawl halfway into the cupboard in order to reach it.

Squatting down behind her and curious as to what she was

doing, Max started to laugh. "Jess, what exactly are you doing down there?"

Startled, she turned to look at him, banging her head against the wall of the cabinet.

"*Ouch...*" Casserole cozy in hand, she backed right into him. This sent him falling back into a sitting position on the floor. And somehow, he managed to take her with him.

Determined to keep her in his arms, he tightened his hold. His mouth settling right next to her ear, she could hear the smile in his voice. "Are you okay?"

In an attempt to ignore the intoxicating feeling of being completely surrounded by him, she closed her eyes. But this didn't stop her voice from coming out all breathless. "I'm fine."

Oh no you're not... not by a long shot.

His lips brushed over the curve of her cheek. "And did you find what you were looking for? Or was this sudden move of yours merely an excuse to avoid responding to what I said?"

"*Max...*"

He chuckled, shaking his head. "Sorry, but I can't help wonder..."

She tried to wiggle out of his arms, but he pulled her even closer. "*Oh, no...* you're not going anywhere. We're going to stay right here until I finally have my say, okay?"

She nodded, and drawn in by the huskiness of his voice, she closed her eyes as he spoke. "Jess, the other night. I acted like an idiot, the accusations I threw at you were way out of line. And I'm so sorry."

He pressed a kiss to the top of her head. "When I realized I'd left my gloves here, I decided to come back. Unfortunately, I was just in time to see this guy show up at your front door and give you a kiss rating pretty high up on the charts. When you went inside, him with a suitcase, I went a little crazy."

His sigh was long, resigned. "I should have turned around and left. Instead I decided to find out what was going on. When I got to the front door, I was just in time to hear everything Chad said about me. None of it complimentary, I got back in my car and left."

He shook his head. "It was only after I got back to the hotel, I wished I had stayed. If only to give you the chance to explain. Instead I let my imagination go wild, thinking the worst."

She sighed, nestling closer to him. "I only answered the door because I thought it was you, looking for your gloves. I didn't ask him to come in. In fact, after he said all those awful things, I told him to leave. I'm embarrassed to say I went a little crazy, throwing his suitcase and coat out into the snow."

She shook her head. "If I could have, I would have thrown him out, too."

She turned her head to gaze up at him. "There was never anything between us. Instead, I think I got caught up in his big plans of becoming this power couple, taking Chicago by a storm. But then I realized I was working twenty-four-seven for something I didn't even want... including Chad."

She sighed. "I believe it was you who told me I was trying to be something I knew in my heart, wasn't really me. Maybe not using these words, but close enough to stick."

He groaned, pulling her closer. "*Oh, boy...* It seems I've said a lot of things, haven't I? And not always good." He pressed another kiss in her hair. "I was so upset with how I'd behaved, after I left the hospital last night, I called my dad."

A slow smile curving her mouth, she looked up at him. "You called your father?"

He nodded. "Yeah, I needed his advice. I wasn't sure what to do next, afraid I'd make a mess of things. After I told him what happened, he laughed. He said it looked like I'd fallen in love and fallen hard."

She could hear the smile in his next words. "He also said he can't wait to meet you."

Her heart had now begun to beat at an insanely crazy rate, anticipation building inside of her.

You need to say something.

But before she could even open her mouth, his mouth dipped dangerously close to hers. "Jess, honey? Look at me."

Their eyes meeting, she was lost.

Completely...

No man had ever looked at her like this before. It was a look that had her ready to agree with whatever he asked, follow him anywhere.

Gently brushing her hair back from her face, he cleared his throat. "Would you like to know what I told him?"

Hardly daring to breathe, she nodded.

A tiny smile hitched the corner of his mouth. "*Ah...* you're speechless. Good... this will give me the chance to say my piece. I told him he was right. On both accounts. I love you, Jess. You have completely turned my life upside down, but in a wonderful way. It's so I can't even remember what it was like before you came along."

He grinned. "Even though you almost killed me in the process. I can only hope you love me, too."

Caught up in her eyes, now the most glorious shade of blue he had ever seen, he waited.

When she relaxed against him with a long sigh, he knew they were going to be okay. Sure enough, she reached up to frame his face in her hands and gave him a brilliant smile.

"*Oh, Max...* I love you, too."

He kissed her. A long, sweet kiss that stole her breath.

It was a kiss that seemed to have no end.

And it was absolutely wonderful...

The kitchen door suddenly flew open.

Laughing as they entered the room, both Jackson and Andy came to an abrupt halt when they saw Max and Jessie on the floor, right in the middle of a kiss.

"*Whoa...*" Jackson's grin couldn't have been any bigger.

An expression of panic on her face Jessie tried to scramble to her feet. But Max put a stop to this, pulling her against him. Wrapping his arms around her, he pressed a kiss to the top of her head before he grinned over at the two boys.

His greeting was casual, as though there was nothing unusual about him and Jessie in the middle of an embrace. And on the kitchen floor, of all places. "Hey, Jackson, Andy... I was wondering where you were. What's up?"

Jackson was still grinning. "Andy's mom picked us up from practice and she's waiting out in the car to see if we need a ride to the community center."

He glanced over at Jessie. "I told her you could take us. Can you?"

Jessie nodded. "Sure... Andy run out and tell your mom we'll bring you home, too."

After Andy left, Jackson's gaze traveled from Max to Jessie before he gave a nod to the floor. "I guess this means you guys aren't fighting anymore?"

They smiled at each other, shaking their heads.

He grinned, glancing over at Max. "Good... I like having you around."

After coming to his feet and pulling Jessie up with him, Max grinned. "Good... because I like being around."

He smiled over at Jessie when Andy came back into the kitchen. "Ready to go?"

Pressing a kiss to his cheek, she handed him the lasagna.

"With you, yes... I'm ready for everything."

CHAPTER 26

$\mathcal{I}$t was the hour right before dawn, such a quiet and peaceful time. When the world almost appears to be taking one final break, not quite ready to welcome a new day.

A taxi pulled up to the hospital's main entrance and a man, dressed in military fatigues, emerged from the back seat.

He gave a long stretch before he gazed around him, a slow smile creasing his face. After he picked up his bag and bid a cheerful farewell to the driver, he went striding into the hospital's main reception area.

He came to a halt, admiring the festive decorations.

There was the silver tinsel tree in the corner, decorated with candy canes and miniature red felt stockings, one for every member of the staff. A silver garland, loaded with ornaments, was draped around the main desk.

He set his bag down on the floor and walked over to the window, where a banner with — This is What Christmas Means to Me — was strung across the top of the glass. Dozens of hand-made paper snowflakes and children's letters to Santa were taped on the glass below.

He was reading one of the letters when a nurse came down the hallway, her eyes on the open folder she was studying.

She glanced up, a big smile lighting up her face when she saw him. "Oh my gosh, Captain McDonnell, you're finally here. Welcome home. Everyone has been pulling for you. Come on, I'll take you to her room."

Chattering the whole time and barely taking a breath between words, he was relieved she didn't seem to expect him to respond. Because, right now, there was only one person he wanted to talk to, be with.

Well, make that two…

After taking the elevator up to the third floor, still chattering non-stop, she led him down the hall to room three-twelve.

She gestured for him to enter. "Go on in. It's a private room so you don't have to worry about disturbing anyone else."

She turned to walk away, then stopped, her words hesitant. "I want you to know, here at the hospital, you and all of the other servicemen are always in our prayers. You sacrifice so much for us and we appreciate it more than you could possibly realize."

He appeared almost embarrassed, shaking his head. "Thank you. And if I wasn't so exhausted right now, I'd personally make the rounds to thank every single one of your staff. But, instead… how about if I just shorten it to *ditto*?"

She laughed. "I'll take it. And now, I'm going to get you a cup of hot cocoa. Along with a couple of homemade cinnamon rolls one of the nurses brought in earlier. Believe me, they're to die for."

He smiled. "If you can pull that off, you'll be my friend for life."

"Okay, I'll be back in a jiffy"

He was still smiling as he quietly made his way into the room. Once his eyes adjusted to the darkness, his gaze traveled over to the bed where Crystal was sound asleep.

For a long moment he didn't move, drinking it all in. After carrying the image of her around in his mind for the past months, it was almost hard for him to believe she was real.

He searched the room, his gaze finally falling on the main reason he had come home. Swiftly making his way over to the bassinet, he reached inside and gently lifted the small bundle into his arms.

He began walking slowly around the room, his words just barely audible in the silence. "Hello, Amelia Jessica. I'm your daddy and I'm so happy to meet you. I'm sorry I wasn't here when you first entered the world, but I want you to know I came as fast as I could."

He stroked her cheek with his fingertip, this bringing her to scrunch up her face in protest. He smiled. "*Ah...* sorry, sweetheart. But I can see, even with the face you just made and in this dim lighting, you are absolutely perfect. I'm willing to bet you're going to be as beautiful as your mommy."

He paused, shaking his head. "I have to confess, this scares me a little. Because right now, I don't even want to think about you going out with boys... or getting married. So, do me a favor, okay? Stay little for as long as you can. And I promise I will always be here for you. Because no matter how old you get, you will always be my baby girl."

Leaning in to press a soft kiss to her forehead, he smiled when she made one of those little baby squeaks before she stretched, settling back in his arms.

"Joe?"

He turned to see Crystal had pulled herself up to a sitting position on the bed and was gazing at him, her eyes wide.

He grinned. "Hey, cupcake... I made it."

"*Oh my gosh... Joe.* It's really you. When I heard your voice, I thought I was only having another dream."

Her face puckering up, she was unable to stop the flood of tears. After she swiped the back of her hand across her face, she gave him a shaky smile. "I'm sorry, I must look a mess."

She watched as he came over to the bed, and lifting her face to his, she fell right into his kiss. A kiss so much better than what she'd held on so tightly in her memory since he'd left.

There was a huskiness in his voice. "You could never be a mess. You are the most beautiful woman I know. And I am so damn happy to see you."

He nodded towards the bed. "Scoot over, hon. So, I can sit next to you."

Once he had settled next to her, he dipped his head to give her another kiss, this one lingering much longer, bringing her to sigh against his mouth.

He gazed down at her. "I can't even begin to tell you how much I missed you, kissing you, holding you...everything." His voice sending a deep tremor through her, this time she was the one to initiate the kiss.

Her head resting against him, she watched as he adjusted Amelia's blanket, loving how he held her so comfortably against him.

She smiled. "So, what do you think of our daughter?"

He smiled down at Amelia. "She's beautiful, Crissy. I just got done telling her this worries me. Another beautiful woman in the family? It almost seems so unfair we should be so lucky."

She laughed, this ending in a sigh. "Oh, Joe... I love you so much. And I'm so glad you're home."

He frowned. "As soon as you told me the doctor was recommending bed rest, I decided I was going to pull every string I could to get home to you. I hounded my commander, giving him every reason I could think of to get his approval. I think he finally gave in only to get me off his back." He shook his head. "It's not fair you've had to handle all of this on your own."

She reached up to stroke his cheek. "It wasn't so bad. Jackson was a big help. He took your lecture very seriously about stepping up to be the man of the house. And Jess... she's been so much help, both in the shop and at home."

She smiled. "And now you'll get to meet Max. He's such a sweetheart. I'm keeping my fingers crossed he might be the one who will finally persuade Jessie to stick around."

He pressed a kiss to her forehead. "I'm glad you had so much support, but I've been thinking... maybe it's time I put in a request to be stationed closer to home. God knows I've got the seniority. Jackson is getting to the age he needs to have his dad around. And more importantly, I need you."

He shook his head. "I can assure you, it was never my intent to marry you and then spend so much time away from you."

After he gave her another kiss, he shrugged. "I don't know what's going to happen, but I can promise you things are going to be different."

He nodded. "A good different."

She leaned over him to look at the clock. "Wow, it's almost morning. I thought it was still the middle of the night. I told them I want to go home today, Christmas Eve day. I already missed the party at the community center last night and I don't want to miss out on anything else. Especially now that you're here."

"I don't see why this can't happen. I want you home, too."

This kiss he was about to give her was interrupted by a light knock on the door. The same nurse who brought him to Crystal entered the room carrying a tray

She was smiling as she set the tray down on the table next to the bed. "Hi, as promised, here are the cinnamon rolls... three of them. Along with two cups of hot cocoa with lots of marshmallows, the only way it should be served. If you want more, you only have to ask."

She peeked over at Amelia, who was still asleep in Joe's arms. "If it's okay with you, I'd like to take her back to the nursery for her routine check. We'll keep her with us for a while, give the two of you some uninterrupted time to catch up."

She grinned at them. "Even though she certainly doesn't look like she's being a bother. I'm sure this is because she is so happy her daddy is home."

After she wheeled Amelia out of the room, Joe gathered Crystal against him, wrapping his arms around her. Burying his face in her hair, he gave a long, contented sigh.

The loud and rumbling growl coming from his stomach was what had him finally pulling away. He chuckled. "As much as I love holding you in my arms, I really want one of those cinnamon rolls. The aroma is killing me and I can't remember the last time I ate."

He ate all three. Well, except for the two big bites he insisted she have.

They talked through the sunrise and up until the doctor stopped by to tell Crystal, as soon as the release papers were filed, she was free to go home.

They talked about everything.

Though she did most of the talking.

But this was okay. He was more than content to let her talk, the soothing sound of her voice washing away everything he wanted to forget about the past year. And he couldn't even begin to explain how much he loved watching the expressions on her face... her beautiful face.

He was so happy to be home.

And lucky...

He was so lucky.

It was going to be a great Christmas.

CHAPTER 27

Christmas is love in action.
Every time we love, every time we give,
it's Christmas.
~Unknown

Curled up on the sofa, Jessie was feeding Amelia her bottle. But it was slow going. Holding the bottle up to check the contents, Jessie smiled down at her, shaking her head. "Amelia, you can't keep falling asleep while you eat. If you keep this up, you'll finish just in time to start on your next bottle."

Crystal came over to sit next to her, reaching for Amelia. "Here, let me try. So far, the only person that can get her to finish her bottle is Joe. I guess they aren't kidding about the special bond between a man and his daughter. Starting from day one, I beginning to believe."

Giving a long stretch, Jessie glanced over at the clock on the mantle. "Wow, it's almost four? I should probably start getting ready. Max sent a text asking if he could come here at five. He said there's something he wants to show me, but promised we'll be back in time for the Christmas Eve service at eight. He wouldn't tell me what it was."

She glanced over at Crystal. "Did he say anything to you?"

Intently watching Amelia drinking her bottle, Crystal shook her head. "*Hmm...* no, not that I remember." She smiled over at Jessie. "So, you two are okay now? Finally on the same page?"

Leaning back against the cushions, Jessie closed her eyes. There was a dreamy smile on her face. "Yeah, we're fine. We're good... really good." She turned her head, gazing over at Chrystal. "I find it so hard to believe we've known each other for only a few weeks. I feel like I've known him forever. And now? I can't imagine my life without him."

She shook her head. "I was so mean to him at first. But he had me so flustered. I couldn't understand how he could be so sure about us. Especially after a friend of his old girlfriend practically threatened me at that wedding we went to."

Crystal sent her a look of surprise. "You never told me about that. What do you mean, threatened?"

"Margo was her name. She made it quite clear Mandy ~ the old girlfriend ~wanted him back. She also told me Max was devastated when he and Mandy broke up. I never told Max about this, since he never really talked about her. But then, I never told him anything about Chad."

She eyed Crystal suspiciously. "*Hmm...* I wonder how he was able to find out about Chad?"

Clearing her throat, Crystal had the grace to look embarrassed. "*Umm...* I may have brought up Chad in one of the conversations I had with Max. But only because, from what you told me, he didn't seem like he was good enough for you. I was worried."

Jessie groaned, shaking her head. "*Crystal...*"

"I know, I know... I'm sorry." Then she grinned. "But everything turned out well in the end. And that's all that matters, right"

She patted Amelia on the back a few more times, getting a dainty little burp from her.

She smiled. "*Finally...*"

One look at Amelia and Jessie laughed. "I think she's already asleep again."

Crystal groaned. "I seriously think I need to give Joe complete responsibility for her. At least for the next three weeks he's on leave."

She glanced over at Jessie. "You haven't even told me how last night went. Who handed out the gifts? Did they ask Max to do it?"

She nodded, answering her own question. "I bet they did. And did you help him? Was there a good crowd? And who won the raffle for the twelve months of coffee cakes I donated?"

Jessie was laughing. "*Whoa*... one thing at a time."

When Crystal stuck her tongue out at her, she shook her head. "I know, I know... you missed being there. Let's start with the cake raffle... Kelly Snow, one of the elementary teachers, won. She was thrilled. When they called her name, she let out a shriek that could've woken the dead. She said she'll wait until after Christmas to contact you."

She smiled. "As soon as we walked in, Susan came over to ask Max to be the honorary Santa. He was so good with all the kids. And as you can imagine, they were so excited to talk to him, both boys and girls. I did help him a little. But it turned out he had plenty of help because three of the guys on the team, Sean, Kevin and Chester, made an appearance. The three were like a comedy team, joking around and teasing the kids. It was a lot of fun. And you should be very proud of Jackson. He and all of his friends helped clean up at the end of the night. And no one even had to ask them. He and Andy almost fell asleep in the car on the way to Andy's house. And you know what a short drive that is. They were exhausted."

Smiling over at the proud expression on Crystal's face, she continued. "The place was packed. From what Susan told me, it was the largest turn out they've ever had. This was because quite a few of the families who came, weren't even from Blossom. She believes once the stolen gifts had been recovered, the word got out there would be more than enough presents to go around. No one went home empty handed, that's for sure."

She laughed. "Milton was there, long face and all. At first, he just moped around. But later in the evening I saw him talking to Kelly, the teacher, and they seemed to be getting along. So, it appears he got over Robin pretty quickly."

Crystal sighed. "Poor Milton. And Bobby. Both of them lost the woman of their dreams. Just like that."

Jessie gave her a look. "Really? Come on, I was never Bobby's woman."

Crystal raised an eyebrow. "Full of yourself, aren't you? Who says I'm referring to you? I think they were both hot for Robin."

Jessie burst out laughing. "I'll have to tell Max. He gets all huffy at the mention of Bobby." She shook her head. "And Bobby would probably be ecstatic if he knew this, the man of the law that he is."

Then she frowned. "The one downfall of the whole evening was the band cancelling at the last minute. Most people probably didn't even miss them, but I was disappointed since Max had promised me a dance."

She sighed. "But even if the band had been there, as swamped as Max was with all his fans, any chance of sharing a dance would've been a long shot."

They were silent for a few moments before Jessie began to laugh. "I probably shouldn't even tell you this, but here goes... do you want to know what Max claimed almost ruined the evening?"

Pressing a kiss to the top of Amelia's head, Crystal groaned. "Oh, no... don't tell me it was something Susan said to him. Or one of the other women on the committee."

"Nope, he was upset he never got any of your lasagna. By the time we had a chance to check out the buffet, it was all gone." She laughed. "You should have seen the expression on his face. You'd think it was the end of the world. Seriously, Crissy, what magical ingredient do you put in the recipe?"

Crystal smiled, shaking her head. "I'm certainly not going to share my secret. You'll have to figure it out yourself."

She sent a pointed look over at the clock. "Speaking of Max, shouldn't you be getting ready? Forty-five minutes and he'll be here."

She grinned, giving Jessie a gentle shove.

"So, go… you don't want to keep the man waiting."

With Amelia comfortably against her shoulder and sound asleep, Crystal was content to stay where she was, watching the flames dancing in the fireplace.

She was feeling very proud of herself. Everyone who accused her of not being able to keep a secret? Well, it was obvious they were wrong.

And this was a very big secret. Life changing, in fact.

She pressed a kiss to Amelia's cheek. "Your mommy is right up there with the best of them, little girl."

A door slammed, bringing Amelia to stir before she uttered a little sigh and went right back to sleep.

Crystal watched as Joe walked into the room, a worried expression coming over his face as he came to sit next to her. "I'm sorry. I forgot what a loud sound that door makes when you close it. I'll have to fix it so it won't wake up this little one."

Reaching over to run his fingertip lightly down Amelia's cheek, he smiled at Crystal. "Did the two of you miss me?"

She leaned over to give him a kiss, ending with a long sigh. "I did. We both did. Very much."

When she moved closer, he put his arm around her. And this is how Jessie found them.

Talking softly, with Amelia sleeping peacefully between them.

CHAPTER 28

This Christmas,
I don't need 5 golden rings.
I only need one...
~ Anonymous

*J*essie and Max had just left Crystal and Joe's house with the promise they would be back in time for the Christmas Eve Mass.

After Max turned the car onto the main road, he sent a quick glance over at Jessie. This happened to be at the exact same time she looked over at him.

He smiled, reaching for her hand. "Joe seems like a really great guy. But, I swear he must have thrown at least a dozen questions at me, one right after the other, before you and Crystal came downstairs. I felt like I was on trial. But I'm pretty sure I passed."

He suddenly looked worried. "At least I think I did."

Jessie laughed. "I'm sure you did fine. When we heard you talking baseball, we knew the two of you would get along just fine. Did he tell you what a big fan he is? He wants to eventually get season's tickets for him and Jackson."

"Umm... I'm not sure exactly what the protocol is with Cleveland when it comes to players and tickets, but I'll see what I can do to make it happen."

He slowed down, turning the car onto a heavily wooded residential street.

After peering out into the darkness, Jessie turned to look at him. "Where in the world are you taking me?"

He sent her a grin. "You'll just have to wait and see. Don't worry, I'm not kidnapping you. Even though it might not be a bad idea. Then I could have you to myself for a while."

She just blurted it out. "I sent in my resignation to the firm today."

This had him slowing the car to a stop before he gazed over at her, a slow smile spreading across his face. "You did... and what made you come to this decision?"

His smile grew even bigger. "But wait... does this have anything to do with me?"

The annoyed expression she wanted to give him just wasn't working. Neither was her nonchalant shrug. Instead she sent him a smile almost as big. "I have a feeling I'm going to regret telling you this, but yes, it had a lot to do with you. But, don't get too big-headed. I also have an interview on the twenty-ninth with a firm in Cleveland. It's the same firm I did an internship the summer before I left for college. When I left, they told me to keep them in mind when I finally passed the bar."

She shook her head, a wry smile on her face. "As you can imagine, at the time, I was appalled. You know, all those big plans I had. Well, yesterday I decided to call them and they wanted to set up an interview right away. I guess one of the partners is leaving because she recently had her fourth child and has decided to take an indefinite leave."

She let out a long breath. *"So...* as it stands right now, I have no job and I will be living with my sister. At least for a while." She smiled over at him. "Maybe I can be the nanny?"

Max was still smiling. "A few days ago you did this. *Hmm...* this is good news. Really good news."

Abruptly tilting his head, he studied her. "But wait a minute... what about my plans to have you do all of my legal work?"

He watched her eyes grow wide, catching her hand right before she went to smack him. Laughing, he brought it to his mouth and pressed a kiss to her fingers. "I'm sorry, I couldn't resist. God, Jess... I love you."

After another kiss, this time to her mouth, he smiled. "As Siri would say, we're almost at our destination. In the meantime, why don't we enjoy all of the Christmas decorations? It looks like they go all out in this neighborhood."

Slowing his speed when they came to a house that looked like it had a million lights in the trees alone, he smiled over at her. "My mom would love this. No matter how many lights my dad puts up, she wants more. But she likes the old-fashioned colored lights. No white lights for her."

She studied him, worry creeping into her voice. "Do you miss your family? I know you said this is the first time you haven't gone home for the holidays."

Slowing the car again, he turned into a driveway. It appeared to be the only house on the street without decorations, the only lighting coming from a porch light and the landscaping lights lining the sidewalk.

He shut off the ignition and turned to her. Even in the darkness, she was drawn in by the warm look in his eyes, a tenderness that had her falling even more in love with him.

"Come here..." His hand framing her face, the rough tone of his voice was enough to send everything inside of her into a frenzy, clamoring to get closer.

Come here? You'd come with him anywhere, anytime.

His lips traveling in a slow trail across her jaw, his mouth captured hers in a sweet, lingering kiss.

Only then did he give her his answer. "I love my family. But right now I love you more and in such a different way." He chuckled, shaking his head. "I don't even know how to go about explaining how I feel. Because, to be honest? I've never felt like this before. I only know it feels right and I don't care where I spend Christmas, as long as it's with you."

He leaned over to give her another kiss before he got out of the car and ran around to open her door. He was smiling as he reached for her hand. "Take my hand. It's sort of icy."

After slipping and sliding on the icy sidewalk, this resulting a quite a bit of laughter and a couple of near falls, they finally made it to the front door.

He unlocked the door and after ushering her inside, he switched on the light.

Completely silent, she gazed around at the open floor plan. There was a large kitchen to one side, with the rest of the room going all the way to the back of the house. This was all windows, giving a view of the wooded backyard.

There was a large wrap around-sofa and a coffee table arranged in front of the stone fireplace. From what she could see, this was the only furniture besides the stools at the kitchen island.

She glanced over at Max to see he was watching her, the intensity of his gaze a sign he was waiting for her to say something.

Unfortunately, she was a little too slow to catch on.

Yep, she had no clue why he brought her to this house

Her smile was tentative. "Max? Is this yours?"

It's ours.

This was the answer he wanted to give, but he knew enough to take things slow.

A smile flitted across his face. Yeah, he got it now… surprises didn't sit well with her.

She needed time.

So, he gave her an answer that could be taken either way. "Well, it could be. It all depends on what we decide."

We?

Now, believe it or not, Jessie was even more confused. Or maybe she wasn't. It was highly possible this was her way of guarding her heart, trying not to read more into what message he could possibly be sending her.

To then have you be disappointed…

Max had no such worries. His confidence was at an all-time high since Jessie gave him the news she wouldn't be returning to Chicago. This explained his smile as he moved to her side. "Here, let me help you with your coat. Then I'll give you a tour."

And this is what he did.

Taking her hand, he started with the kitchen. Newly remodeled, it had enough gadgets and appliances for even the fussiest gourmet chef.

Running her hand over the quartz countertop, she smiled over at him. "Crystal would die for a kitchen like this."

He nodded. "*Ah*…I bet she would. But I'm more interested to know what you think."

Slowly gazing around the room, she shook her head. "It's beautiful. A dream kitchen."

Pressing a kiss to her cheek and her hand back in his, they moved on to the guest room with its' own private bath, followed by a quick look at the other two bedrooms and a room that had been turned into an office.

But it was the master bedroom, with the high ceiling and large windows, that Jessie fell in love with. Even though she claimed she wouldn't know what to do with so much space, the en suite bathroom almost as big as the whole upstairs of Crystal and Joe's house.

The last part of the tour took them to the lower level. A combination media and game room it was the ultimate man cave.

Once they were back upstairs, he pulled her with him into the middle of the room. Taking both her hands in his, he searched her face. "So, what do you think?"

The earnest expression on his face had her giving him a kiss on his cheek. "It's a beautiful house."

Then, believe it or not, she slowly gazed around the room, the practical part of her suddenly taking over. "You do realize you would have to buy more furniture." She glanced over at the windows overlooking the backyard, shaking her head. "And wouldn't you want some kind of window coverings for privacy? Not that you have anything to hide. But—"

He pressed his fingers to her lips. "*Shh...* We don't need to worry about those things now. There is something so much more important I'd like to know... would you consider living here?"

"Me? Live here?"

He sighed and framing her face in his hands, he nodded. "Yes, Jess... I want you to live here... with me."

Her heart dropped to her stomach.

He wants you to live with him? Just move right in?

But why would he even think she'd agree to this? She searched his face, hoping to see something, *anything* that would better explain what he said.

But she saw only his smile.

She took a deep breath. "So... let me get this right...you're asking me to move in with you?"

And this is when he understood what was happening, why this moment he'd hoped would be one they'd always remember, had now turned into one he wished they could forget.

Or at least have a chance to start over.

Yeah, you'd give anything to walk out the door and do it all again.

"No, no, no..." Dropping his hands from her face, he reached into his jean's pockets. A look of pure panic flashing across his face, he frantically began patting the rest of his pockets before he went sprinting over to grab his coat, searching those pockets as well.

Before she could even ask him what he was doing, he gave a

triumphant laugh and was back standing in front of her. He shook his head. "Jess, I want you to forget about everything I said. Instead, let's start over. Okay?"

Her eyes on what he was holding in his hand, she put her hand to her mouth, nodding like crazy.

She watched as he slowly went down to one knee, the whole time his gaze holding hers.

Holding up the small jeweler's box, he nervously cleared his throat.

"Jessica Louise Carter..." Here, he chuckled at her look of surprise. "I asked Crystal for your middle name. After all, I want to do this right."

She nodded, something she couldn't seem to stop doing.

This was enough to have him go on. "I don't know how it happened... nor do I know how I got so lucky, finding you like I did. What I do know is I love you and I want to share my life with you. Marry me, Jess...?"

She reached out to him. But it was her eyes, now every shade of blue he could ever ask for and shining with so much love, that gave him his answer. Even before she was finally able to say the words he wanted to hear.

"Oh, Max... *yes, yes, yes...* of course I'll marry you."

They almost didn't make it in time for the Christmas Eve Mass.

CHAPTER 29

You are the jingle to my bells,
the winter to my wonderland,
the milk to my cookie and the star on my tree.
~ Anonymous

*S*nowflakes were beginning to drift down from the sky when Jessie and Max finally made their escape from the crowded gathering room of the church.

Max had learned very quickly, when someone gets engaged in Blossom Falls, it's big news. If the engagement takes place on Christmas Eve, it's even better.

And if it just so happens a celebrity of some kind is involved? Why, it couldn't get any more exciting than this.

As soon as the service was over, they had been mobbed, questions and well intended advice coming at them from all directions. So, the first chance they got, they grabbed their coats and left.

But this was also made possible because Amelia was there to steal some of the limelight. Everyone wanted to see the Christmas baby, this the title bestowed on Amelia, and one that would be a part of her for life.

Since this would be her first Christmas, Crystal had insisted they bring her to church with them. They were a family, she said, and as long as Amelia was all bundled up, she would be fine.

At first, Joe wasn't sure about this. But, like Jackson, he knew once Crystal made her mind up about something, there was no stopping her.

As Crystal predicted, Amelia was fine. Like a little angel, she slept throughout the entire service, not a single peep coming from her.

Joe also found he enjoyed showing her off to everyone.

Now standing on the steps to the church and holding her arms up to the sky, Jessie smiled over at Max. "Isn't it absolutely beautiful? This is exactly how Christmas Eve should be... the snow, the lights, the decorations. All of the shopping and hectic planning done, leaving everything now so hushed and peaceful."

Max reached for her hand.

He was smiling. But then it seems like he hadn't stopped smiling ever since he slipped the ring on her finger.

He still couldn't believe she had resigned from her job in Chicago. This had been the reason he'd held out on finalizing the deal on the house. He had already decided he would gladly have a home base in Chicago if this is where Jessie felt her career was headed.

So now, he had even more of a reason to smile.

He leaned over to kiss her cheek. "It is perfect, isn't it? But then, ever since you tried to run me over..." As he thought would happen, she swiftly glanced over at him, ready to defend herself.

But as a lawyer, this was more than understandable.

Instead, laughter bubbling up in her throat, she reached up to link her fingers behind his neck. "You are never going to let me forget that, are you? Again, I did not hit you. I stopped in plenty of time." She shook her head. "I was in complete control."

This, of course was a lie. Because her heart had never been in her control.

No, she had willingly given it to him.

He pulled her against him, pressing a kiss in her hair. "But you didn't let me finish. What I was going to say... you, your family, Christmas baby Amelia, you saying yes to my proposal and our new house? All of these add up to the best Christmas I've ever had. And I can't wait for what's in store for us over the next seventy-five years or so."

He could see she appeared to have stopped listening to him. And he knew this was because she was trying to figure out if she had heard him right. "*Our* new house? You bought the house?"

She was gazing up at him, giving him a chance to get lost in her eyes. That they were a beautiful combination of every possible shade of blue, he knew she approved.

Resting his forehead against hers, he nodded. "Yes, if you agree, it is officially ours."

"Oh, Max... of course, I agree. I loved everything about the house. But then I'd live anywhere with you." She framed his face in her hands. "I love you, Max Kirby. And that you love me, too, is the best Christmas gift I could ever get."

She suddenly grinned. "So, do you consider this a home run kind of moment?"

A teasing glint in his eyes, he shook his head. "A home run? *Hmm*... I don't think that can even begin to explain how I feel about you."

Pressing a soft kiss to his mouth, she smiled. "No?"

For a few moments, he was lost... her eyes, her beautiful eyes, pulling him in. Then he smiled, shaking his head. "*No*... I'd have to say this is more like a grand slam kind of Christmas. I love you, Jess."

"I love you, too."

He had just lowered his head to kiss her when the church bells began to chime. Stepping back, he was smiling as he reached for her hand. "I do believe this would be the perfect time and place to share our first dance. So... will you do me the honor?"

So... they danced.

To the glorious sound of the church bells, while snowflakes drifted like confetti in a celebration around them.

It was the perfect first dance.

"Hey, you two... wait for us." This yell was followed by a snowball landing right by their feet.

Hand in hand, they waited for Crystal, Joe, Jackson and their new littlest angel, Amelia, to join them.

They all agreed.

It was the best Christmas Eve... *ever*.

A few days later, Max and Jessie decided to do a little shopping in Blossom Falls. It was while Jessie was waiting in line to pay for a pair of baby booties she had picked out for Amelia, Max found something he knew he had to get for Jessie. It was a plaque. And on it was this quote.

You give me that bottom of the ninth ~
last at bat ~ tied game ~ full of butterflies ~
grand slam ~ kind of feeling.

It was perfect.

Later while they were sharing a pizza in Rosie's Italian Kitchen, he gave it to her. This, he told her, was how she made him feel. This, and so much more.

They haven't decided yet where they're going to hang it in their new house. But they're not worried.

They have a lifetime to think about it.

❄

It's Coffee Cake Time...

It is completely understandable you now want to run to your kitchen and whip up a coffee cake.

This is exactly what Crystal predicted. So, she has been generous enough to allow one of her recipes to be included in this book. A warning ~ Joe, Jackson and Max have been known to fight over the last piece. It's also a customer favorite.

And if you're thinking of claiming the recipe as your own? Crystal wants you to remember she has one of the best lawyers around to take on the case.

P.S. Jessie still hasn't been able to get the recipe from Crystal for her lasagna. But as Max told her, this probably isn't going to happen. At least not for a long time.

Crystal's Caramel Apple Pecan Coffee Cake:

Filling:
    2 cups diced peeled tart apples (Granny Smith)
    1/2 cup chopped pecans, lightly toasted
    1/3 cup light brown sugar
    2 tablespoons butter, melted
    2 teaspoons ground cinnamon

Cake:
    2 cups all-purpose flour
    1 teaspoon baking powder
    ¼ teaspoon baking soda
    ½ teaspoon salt
    8 tablespoons butter, softened
    1 cup sugar
    2 large eggs, room temperature
    1 cup sour cream

Caramel Sauce:

6 tablespoons butter
3/4 cup brown sugar
3 tablespoons half-and-half
A pinch of salt
1 teaspoon vanilla

Garnish:

1/2 cup chopped pecans, lightly toasted
(Optional)

Directions:

1. Preheat the oven to 350°F. Grease and
flour a 9-1/2" tube-pan.
2. Combine the filling ingredients. Set
aside.
3. For the cake, whisk together the flour,
baking powder, baking soda, and salt. Set
aside.
4. In a large mixing bowl, beat the butter,
sugar and eggs for 2 to 3 minutes or until
light and fluffy.
5. Add the flour mixture to the butter
mixture alternately with the sour cream,
beating at low speed to combine after
each addition.
6. Spoon half of the batter into floured
tube pan and top with half of the filling.
Repeat layers.
7. Bake at 350° for 35 to 45 minutes or
until a toothpick inserted in the center
comes out clean. Transfer the cake to a
pan) and prepare the caramel sauce.
8. To make the sauce, melt butter in a

small heavy saucepan.

9. Whisk in the brown sugar, half and half and salt. Cook until mixture comes to a boil. Continue whisking for 3 to 4 minutes or until mixture starts to thicken.

10. Add in vanilla, whisking about a minute longer before removing from heat. Brush about 1/4 cup of the sauce over the top of the cake still in pan.

11. Let the cake sit for 15-20 minutes to absorb the sauce.

12. Turn the cake out onto a platter, then drizzle the remaining sauce over the cake. If desired, garnish with toasted chopped pecans. Let stand until cool (at least 1 hour) before slicing.

Enjoy!

ABOUT THE AUTHOR

L. B. Joyce lives in Chagrin Falls, Ohio. A freelance artist by day, with designing Christmas ornaments her specialty, she's also a writer by night. She loves getting lost in a good book, has redecorated almost every room in her house more times than she'd like to admit, loves baking up a storm in her kitchen, hates housework with a passion and will drive just about anywhere because of her fear of flying.

To keep up with all of the news about this book, along with the first eight novels of the series, Twelve Months, Twelve Love Stories ~ A Million Decembers, For the Love of July, February's Angel, Promise Me November, An Unexpected June. A January to Remember, September's Moonlight Serenade, and Goodbye Heartbreak, Hello May - check out the website/blog at:

https://www.lbjoyceauthor.com

Or visit on Facebook:

https://www.facebook.com/LBJoyceAuthor/

You can also email her at: lbjoyce12@gmail.com

She would love to hear from you!

Cover by Soxsational Cover Art